Praise for *The Mountain Rats*

Your stories evoked much emotion for me, which I think is what a writer wants. You wrote about things very close to me. Your perseverance to make the Catskills house a reality is awesome.

Sandra Foley, Harbor View Book Club leader

I spent my childhood in the Catskills. Your story is not only informative, it's beautifully written. I truly loved your stories.

Adrienne Leslie, author of *Alice Again* and two other novels

I have been teaching literature at the Korea Daily Newspaper's cultural center (JoongAng Ilbo, NY) for 15 years. He is one of the most talented students. He is a gifted writer. His thinking is clear and determined. But he writes with poise and warmth. His stories are evocative and touching.

Jeongki Kim, poet

When I think of Boklim Choi, three words come into my mind: generosity, intelligence, and dedication. As a former president of the Korean American Scholarship Foundation Northeastern region, he has been very generous with his time and with his financial support. When I served as the chairman of KASF, his provocative, intelligent mind brought fresh new ideas to enrich our organization. Now he has created short stories that reflect his intelligence in this book. As I surmised, his stories are very interesting and imaginative, stimulating our minds with a kind of suspense that provokes the reader—a page-turner. I am certain that you will enjoy reading his stories.

Chung Hun Lee, judge
Municipal Court of Duluth
Gwinnett County, Georgia

The Mountain Rats

For [illegible]

Thanks for the support

Best Wishes,

9-22-2014

Bokim Choi

The Mountain Rats

A collection of short stories by

Boklim Choi

The Mountain Rats

Published in the United States of America by Seoul Selection USA, Inc.
4199 Campus Dr., Suite 550
Irvine, CA 92612, USA
Tel: 949-509-6584
Fax: 949-509-6599
E-mail: publisher@seoulselection.com
Website: www.seoulselection.com

ISBN: 978-1-62412-030-5 51500
Library of Congress Control Number: 2014946358

Printed in the Republic of Korea

Although partially inspired by real people and events, the following collection of short stories is a work of pure fiction, and should be read as such.

Contents

Foreword

Chance encounters are the stuff that novels are made of. It's rare that real, enduring respect and affection are born out of random events, but they were when I met journalist, poet, and short story writer Boklim (Peter) Choi. We were seated next to each other at a Korean-American charity dinner. I was there to talk about my term as New York's educational envoy to Korea and visit to the DMZ. My personal journey from teacher to writer was of great interest to the Korean-American community. I'm a green-eyed European-American who, by chance, made a career in teaching new Korean-Americans. Since I had grown up in an extended family, with my grandmother having the final say and my parents caring for her through her final days, I gravitated to a culture that echoed my own respect for elders.

I had not intended to spend most of the evening enraptured by only one tablemate, but by the second course, I was totally charmed by the vibrant man seated at my left. At that time, I was writing impact panel pieces for a New York newspaper and wished I had more time to talk to Mr. Choi about his views on recent events. He quickly turned the tables on me with his analytical thinking and journalistic skills. I was soon opening my heart to this stranger about my rainy morning in the Demilitarized Zone when I spied a crane take flight from the rushes between North and South Korea, and wept for a nation where birds were free to fly from south to north and back again, but people were not. It was a painful memory I hadn't shared with anyone until Peter's skillful investigation brought it forth.

On a chilly morning at the DMZ, I made a silent promise to return to the United States as an advocate for Korean-American issues. I wrote three novels for non-Koreans to better enhance their understanding of a great people with a sorrowful history. I also became a board member at the Korean-American Scholarship Foundation, but have never been able to keep up with Peter's tireless work ethic. While I still struggle with my Korean, Peter is capable of enlightening and illuminating in two languages. As an immigrant writer, he is fascinated by the more than 180 languages spoken in New York City and believes each new immigrant arrives with a cultural past and a story to tell. His short story collection, titled *The Mountain Rats*, opens a window that looks out onto a plain of Koreans and Korean-Americans, each with his or her own cultural schema. Although his short stories are written in English for all audiences, they wriggle and bore into our souls like intricate Joseon poetry that whispers to us long after the book is closed.

An avid reader with an unquenchable thirst for universal questions, he surprised me recently by asking for the definition of the antebellum term basket name, which he had run across in his readings. In minutes, the two of us were trying out context clues and checking online till we knew that a basket name was the name given to a baby by its slave mother as opposed to the name it would receive from its master. How prophetic that two writers committed to Korean causes should find a connection linking historic slavery in the American South to the *nobi* of ancient Korea. I thoroughly enjoyed that afternoon with the passionate and compassionate Boklim Choi. As a proponent of investigative learning, I know that Boklim, if he chose to, could easily be a respected and beloved teacher.

Sympathetic and solicitous, Boklim isn't satisfied by details. His power of keen observation will leave him sleepless as he explores what he calls the other side of facts to arrive at the truth. His extraordinary tenacity has not only served him well as a journalist, it has given him an armature for his poetry and short story writing. Peter avoids what he calls dry words, the mundane language a lesser writer may choose rather than get to the core of his characters. Peter's work never fails to move his readers' hearts.

Inspired by actual events in Virginia, Choi's *A Meeting of Hearts* is a melancholy yet heartening story of an American man who, much to the consternation of his children, leaves his ten million dollar estate to his second wife, a Korean-American nurse. The clash between Western lack of respect for elders and Korean sympathy for the sick and aged is a tale that will leave readers with new perspectives and a deeper understanding of cultural differences.

Another of Boklim's stories, *The Last Dinner*, is of particular interest to me, since he and I now meet often as KASF board members. I paid homage to the supportive help for Korean and Korean-American students in my novel *Alice Again* by creating a fictional charity. Boklim went further by using his long relationship with the Foundation to force his readers to question our personal definitions of death.

In this tender account, the author and central characters speak with one voice. Readers will weep, as I did, when Choi's protagonist confesses his sins, asks for forgiveness, and makes his final attempt at redemption. Rather than have a customary funeral, the main character allows himself a final goodbye before death. This unconventional look at the meaning of legacy is a powerful and respectful homage to The Korean American Scholarship

Foundation. I hasten to note that just before publishing his collection, Boklim confided that he and his daughter both cried as they re-read *The Last Dinner.*

Asking me to select a favorite of Boklim's beautiful stories is like asking a mother to point to her prettiest child, but *The Mountain Rats*, the title story, brought me to my own childhood summers in upstate New York. His attention to the quietus of the woods is perfection. Still, I can't recall a more uplifting reading experience than when I read *A Tale of Two Widows.* The brutality of 9/11 plays a perfect counterpoint to the tenacity of Choi's characters. This journey from wife to widow to wife is cataloged with respect and awe.

I trust that Boklim's collection is just his first step on a long road of recording the Korean immigrant experience for future generations. He is a tenacious writer who believes it's his responsibility as a first generation journalist-writer to record immigrant accounts. I believe he is the perfect writer for the job.

Looking back on our first meeting, I wonder if either of us could have sensed a lasting friendship in our future. Even if we did not expect to be fellow colleagues, friends, and writers, I stand by my first impressions. I knew he was an exceptional man with more than one poignant story inside him. His extraordinary first collection, *The Mountain Rats*, has proven me right.

Adrienne Leslie

Adrienne Leslie, author of the novel *Alice Again*. A former teacher turned writer, Adrienne Leslie has been interested in Korean and Korean-American issues since childhood, and has dedicated herself to both learning and writing about them.

A Meeting of Hearts

The dim light of dawn reached the hospital bed where Tom Curtis lay half asleep. He glanced out the window and tried to get up, but a sharp pain in his chest stopped him

He was frustrated and angry with himself. For the first time in his life he felt vulnerable. About two hours later, a nurse knocked on the door and entered with a smiling but worried face. He barely moved. She was not the same nurse that he had seen the past several days.

"Good morning, Mr. Curtis. How do you feel

this morning?" He didn't answer. He just stared and studied her face and its features. She looked unfamiliar. But he welcomed her warm, inviting, and calm presence.

"My name is Young, and I'm your new nurse. Today is my first day at work and you're the first patient on my shift," she said.

"You are Young and you look young," he said.

"I may be younger than you, but I feel old. By the way, are you okay, Mr. Curtis?" she asked in a soft voice. "You look a little pale, but you'll be fine soon. It takes time. The surgery was a success. You'll regain your strength soon." He was greatly relieved and enormously encouraged. The nurse checked his pulse rate and blood pressure.

"I'll be back in two hours, and the doctor will visit you in the morning. Mr. Curtis, don't worry. You'll be fine." She closed the door behind her and quietly left the room.

Solitude and emptiness remained as he sat there alone. He looked at the calendar. It was June 21, the summer solstice, the longest day of the year. Summer had finally arrived. It was all downhill from here.

Daylight hours were about to shrink. He suddenly felt sadness and realized nobody was with him. He was all alone. Too many things had happened in the last several months.

Tom Curtis was a fifty-six-year-old college professor. He taught English at Stony Brook University. Literature had been his love since childhood. He inherited his passion for art from his father. His father, Ben Curtis, was a high school English teacher. His study was filled with rare books, mostly classics, philosophy, and history books. Ben Curtis loved to talk about literature with Tom, his only son. Tom had worked as an editor of the school newspaper. He had written poems and short stories and was a true critic. His father was enormously proud. After graduating high school with honors, Tom studied literature at Yale, where he became the art editor of the Yale Daily News.

Tom met Carol Randolph at Yale. She was a double major in sociology and history. She was brilliant, cool, and articulate—and a very attractive woman. Her father was a partner at a prestigious law firm in

Manhattan. Her family had a gorgeous apartment on Park Avenue and a mansion in Greenwich, Connecticut. After graduating from Yale, Tom was accepted at Dartmouth in a master's and doctoral program in English. He received his doctorate in four years. Meanwhile, Carol entered Yale Law School, received her J.D. degree, and passed the New York bar examination. Tom and Carol started dating after they both got jobs: Tom as an assistant professor at Stony Brook and Carol as an assistant district attorney in Manhattan. After three years, they got married. Tom was thirty and Carol was twenty-eight.

Carol had a sharp mind. She had made a name for herself as a top prosecutor taking on some of the toughest cases. She was highly regarded by Joe McCarthy, the Manhattan district attorney. Whenever he had high-profile cases, she was the first one considered. She had handled two sensational cases. One was the high-stakes trial of an accused serial killer. She had spent a great deal of time working on this case, not only at the office but also at home. She also worked weekends, going through boxes of forensic reports and evidence, working on an opening statement for the trial, and organizing the prosecution down to the last detail. Her efforts earned a conviction verdict from the jury. Carol's other case was a fraud and conspiracy charge against a large investment firm. The company had embezzled tens of millions of dollars from innocent investors. Carol fought for this case for two years and was finally awarded a guilty verdict. With these two world-known cases under her belt, Carol became a major player in the legal community. After serving six years for the Manhattan DA, she received an offer to be a partner at a prestigious law firm and she joined. Her salary jumped from a mere six figures to more than a million dollars. She made almost ten times more than her husband. Tom and Carol purchased a three-bedroom apartment near Central Park, and a one-acre colonial house in Sands Point, Long Island.

Carol and Tom were the ideal couple until they realized that they had irreconcilable differences. Carol was a bright, capable lawyer. She was thorough, formidably cool, and efficient. She didn't pay too much attention to her family, including Tom. Even though she was meticulous when dealing with legal issues, for domestic matters, she scarcely cared. When Tom said he was hungry, she would say, "Why don't we go out to eat?" When Tom needed a clean shirt, she would say, "Go to the cleaners." When Tom complained about sickness, she would say, "Go see a doctor. I'm not a doctor." Though she didn't explicitly ask Tom not to bother her, she clearly implied it. Taking care of her family had never been her priority. She cared most about her job. She seldom came to their Long Island home. They lived virtually separate lives. Tom didn't complain, for he knew she wouldn't care anyway. They had remained an odd couple for almost twenty years.

The couple had a son, Michael, and a daughter, Jamie. When their kids graduated from college and got jobs, Tom and Carol realized that they had a reached a breaking point. They reluctantly recognized that the gulf between them was too wide to be bridged. They had never really fit into each other's way of life. It all happened like a bad movie—a real-life nightmare. Tom thought she had stolen all of his dreams, and Carol believed that Tom had never tried hard enough to salvage their marriage. They agreed to separate, and finally divorced. That was three years ago. Carol took her Manhattan apartment and Tom remained in Sands Point. Tom was fifty-three, and Carol was fifty-one. More than twenty years of marriage had come to an end. Tom sobbed; Carol didn't. She was calm, took it like another legal case, and parted from him.

Tom lived in an old colonial house with tall white columns, a stately entrance, an ornate gate, and a long driveway leading up to the house. It was not a big house, smaller than most of the surrounding houses. It had three bedrooms, a study, and a guest room. The house sat on the prettiest part of Sands Point. It was not on the immediate waterfront, but close enough to watch the seagulls flying and smell the gentle breeze coming from the North Shore. In the winter, Tom could hear the rage of the wind. The house was filled with a sense of tradition—antiques and grandeur, but no warmth. After Carol moved out, the house felt empty, too big for a single man. It was dead quiet. Nobody paid a visit, no one called, not a single stray dog or cat could be found roaming nearby the house.

Tom spent most of his time in the house but was never much of a caretaker. His house turned into a neglected ghost house and an embarrassment to the upscale neighborhood. He needed somebody to take care of the house and him. He hired a housekeeper to make meals for him and do laundry and housework. Tom also hired a gardener to cut the grass in the summer and shovel the snow in the winter. Even through all his ordeals, Tom was a handsome, distinguished-looking man. He was a polite and charming gentleman. He seldom lost his temper. He was serious, conservative, and gracious. Some people may have thought him aloof because he didn't talk much and didn't try to placate others. He was an intelligent and emotional person.

Carol shut him out after the divorce. She closed that chapter of her life. Tom had no choice. He had to adjust to his changed circumstances. Their son, Michael, was a lawyer in Los Angeles. He, like his mother, was cool, logical, calculating, and never showed his emotions. Jamie studied art management at Columbia University and worked for the Smithsonian in the District of Columbia. She was like her father—warm, caring, and compassionate. They were not happy with their parents' divorce but accepted their decision. Michael was out of touch, but Jamie was in close contact with her parents.

After the painful separation, Tom felt his health had deteriorated. He was dizzy at times, and there was a tightening in his chest, but he didn't pay much attention to his symptoms, mainly because he had no one to complain to. In truth, however, he was in denial; something terrible happened to him quite suddenly two weeks prior. It was Saturday morning. He collapsed during his morning exercise and lost consciousness. If the housekeeper hadn't called him for breakfast, he might have died. An ambulance was rushed in and he was taken to St. Francis Hospital in Port Washington. He was in critical condition, but survived after double-bypass heart surgery.

After a gentle knock, Dr. Fisher entered the room. He was smiling. "How do you feel, Mr. Curtis? Your progress is excellent. As I told you, the surgery was successful. There's a bit of damage to your heart muscle, but it's not extensive. You'll fully recover if you take good care of yourself. By the way, you have a new nurse today. She is excellent and beautiful. We used to work together at North Shore Hospital. Everybody loved her. She is perceptive, caring, and has a good heart—I mean, a good personality."

"I saw her briefly this morning. I got a good feeling," Tom said.

"Since everything is okay, you can leave the hospital whenever you want after Friday. Stay two more days. Do you have someone to take care of you?" the doctor asked.

"I have a housekeeper, though I am not sure she is good enough," Tom said warily.

The nurse entered Tom's room. "Mr. Curtis, the doctor told me you are going home soon. I am sure you are happy to go back to your family. You've been here almost a week."

"I'm not sure if I'm happy to be discharged, but I guess I'm not allowed to stay any longer. My insurance won't cover it. Dr. Fisher said that you are a highly respected nurse and I have no doubt in my mind. You're different. While other nurses work like robots, you are a true nurse."

"Mr. Curtis, that's not true. What are you saying?

We all work hard and I am the same as the others."

"I don't think all nurses were created equal. However, I had no problem with the other nurses. I just believe that you are exceptional. By the way, what country are you from?"

"I am Korean. I got my nursing education in Korea. That's why I speak with an accent."

"Oh, your English is close to native. I am an English professor. Your vocabulary is good and grammatically correct. I think you studied at school or you read a lot," Tom said.

"Yes, I studied English literature at Hofstra University. But I am not quite there yet."

"You have a bit of an accent, but that's okay. If people don't understand you, it's not your fault. It's their problem."

"Thanks, you are regaining your strength now. Your complexion shows that. You'll be getting better every day."

"Thanks, Young, I'll will miss you. I may ..." He didn't finish what he wanted to say. She left quietly. The door closed and he was lonely again. Tom was thinking about the Korean nurse. She was not tall, but not short either. She was lean. Her skin looked exceptionally white for an Asian woman, almost as white as Caucasian women. She had a nice smile, but her smile was not wide. She looked shy, pure, and genuine. She was pretty. She had a passion that was almost entrancing. She seemed to have a beautiful mind, unspoiled by lust and jealousy. She was not the average nurse. She did possess a heart.

It was Saturday morning and it was pouring. The rain started early in the morning and grew in intensity as the day wore on. Tom awoke around six in the morning and looked around the room where he had stayed for the last seven days. After breakfast, he barely had time to dress. He should have been happy to go home, but he was not. Nobody was waiting for him. He would dearly miss the nurse that was caring for him. He thought, "I don't want to leave you." Young was beside him. His watery eyes gazed at her. He wanted to ask her whether she would do private care if he needed it. He stopped. At ten o'clock Tom was brought down by wheelchair to the hospital lobby and a limousine arrived for him. Young was surprised that none of his family members came to pick him up. The driver opened the door and Tom entered the back seat. Tom and Young's eyes met. He was leaving behind a thousand words. Tom extended his hands to her and said, "I'll miss you. Hopefully …" He didn't finish his sentence. Young was weeping. "Mr. Curtis, take care. You'll be okay. I'll pray for you. If you really need me …" The limousine departed through the heavy rain.

Young was exhausted when she entered her apartment that evening. Tom had left a strong impression. "He is a gentleman," she thought. "He looks lonely and withdrawn, but he always kept his decency and composure. He is gracious. He deserves more love from his family. Where is the family? Why a limo? Can he really take care of himself? If nobody does …" She wanted to provide her kindness, warmth, and compassion to him. She was surprised to realize that she had lots of emotion for him. It was vague, but wasn't an illusion.

It was the same house Tom had lived in for the last twenty years, but when he arrived home from the hospital, it looked like a strange place. The housekeeper greeted him and asked him what he wanted for dinner. He couldn't answer. He had lost his appetite and didn't know what he wanted to eat. The phone rang. It was Jamie. "Dad, I'm very sorry. I should have picked you up. The conference is over and I'll be home this weekend. Dad, how do you feel?"

"I feel much better. Thanks, Jamie. You are the only one who cares."

"Dad, don't feel bad. You're independent and strong. You'll be fine. I'll see you soon."

Tom went to his bedroom and laid his weary body down. He couldn't sleep. He missed Young. He knew that she was not available.

Jamie arrived that weekend. She was not like her mother. She had been a good daughter, even more caring now because her beloved father was sick.

A few days after Tom was discharged, Dr. Fisher was looking for Young. "Young, you are so popular. Every patient wants you. Tom called me the other day. He wanted me to ask you whether you would work as a private nurse for him. He was very cautious. He thought that you might not be an easy nurse to ask."

"Why me? There are lots of good nurses here. I've seldom worked for extra money. I am not a big spender. I don't have a family to support, as you know."

"It's not about the money. It's about the care. He needs your care. If you don't want his money, you can work for nothing. He needs you to help him not only with his physical recovery, but also for his emotional stability. You know people are susceptible to depression after heart attacks. Can I pass on your contact information to him?" Young couldn't refuse. She had been worried about his condition for the past few days.

Tom sent a limousine for Young. When the limo approached his house, nothing looked familiar to her as she gazed out the window. There was a wide expanse of grounds and the driveway was long and winding. Tom was waiting on the porch. He looked pale, but managed a smile. He opened the back door and said, "Thanks, Young. I am happy to see you again. Please feel free to ask for anything you need." Tom treated her as if she were a special guest, not a visiting nurse. Young was a bit confused, but didn't say anything. Tom led her into a living room that was opulent and full of antiques. There was a beautiful chandelier in the adjoining dining room. The space had a delicate scent and she noticed that the curtains were adorned with silk tassels. Everything in the living room was impeccable and in perfect order, but something was missing. There was no vestige of human warmth. It was empty, chilly, and eerily silent. The house was like a small museum. It didn't feel like a place where she could walk around in jeans and bare feet. The housekeeper brought a tray with drinks and fruit. She looked to be in her sixties and as if she had a tender heart. Tom and Young looked at each other. He was very happy. His sick, gloomy face was gone. It was beaming. Young realized why he needed her so earnestly.

Young visited Tom's residence three days a week: three hours on Wednesdays and Fridays, and two hours on Saturdays. Whenever she came, he was always ready to go out for a walk, and always reported his condition. Young checked his medications, told him what to eat, and helped him plan his exercise. They usually walked together for an hour around the neighborhood. Some of the neighbors would say hello, but they didn't ask Tom who she was. They probably thought that she was his girlfriend. One day Tom said to Young, "Marriage is kind of a contract. Carol and I couldn't fulfill our contract with dignity, so we agreed to terminate it. Now I am as free as a bird. But sometimes I feel empty, abandoned, and lost in the world."

"I have that feeling occasionally. I am not as withdrawn as you are, because I've never had any family. When I feel lonely, I travel. I've already booked a winter trip to Hawaii."

"Hawaii? Where in Hawaii? I've been to Maui and the other islands, but never the Big Island."

"Oh, I am going there in mid-January for ten days."

"Are you going with a group or on your own?"

"With a group. I made a reservation through Liberty Travel. You probably will not need me to care for you by then. You're almost back to normal now."

"I'll miss you. And I'll need you even when I'm fully recovered, not necessarily as a nurse but as a friend." They laughed and went out for dinner. It was November. Though it was late fall, it felt like early winter. The color of the ocean had changed and the windswept water brought cold air into Tom's house. Darkness fell faster after Daylight Savings Time had ended.

Young came one day and said she was not coming anymore. "Tom, you don't need me anymore. I had a good time with you. You're a true gentleman. I've helped lots of patients, but you're the most respectable and unpretentious one. I'll miss you. But I have to leave you. I have my own life to live." Tom couldn't say anything. Young was more than a nurse to him. She was his friend, his soul mate. But he had no right to not let her go. When she left his house, he handed her an envelope.

"Mr. Curtis, I didn't come here to make money. I don't need a lot of money. I lead a modest life. You can buy other nurses, but not me. I came here because I cared for you and liked you." Tom couldn't say a word. He extended his arms and hugged her. He wanted to kiss her, but he knew she would turn away from him.

Christmas season is always bustling and exciting. St. Francis Hospital was elegantly decorated and the hospital staff exchanged gifts. Since Young didn't have many friends, she didn't give or receive many presents. She felt a bit alienated from the others. On December 22, when she finished her shift, the nursing office handed her a small package. It was from Tom. She didn't want to open it there, so she waited until she brought it home. When she unwrapped the package, she was surprised. There was a glittering ring with a small diamond. She had no idea what its value was. It looked so nice that she couldn't even think to return it to him. There was a handwritten note along with it:

Dear Young,

I can't find words to let you know how much I appreciate what you've done for me. Please accept this gift. By the way, I am going to the Big

Island the same week you will be there. I hope you don't mind. I booked it through Liberty Travel. Have a wonderful holiday.

God bless you,
Tom

Tom and Young toured Hawaii's Big Island together that January. The group arrived at about eight o'clock in the evening. The sun was setting in a blaze of fiery glory. The island loomed darkly, and white clouds lingered over the mountains against the pink-lavender sky. Soon the moon rose, and people could see silver reflections on the dark waters. After checking into their hotel rooms, Tom and Young joined the rest of the group for dinner. Tom had reserved his own room and Young was sharing her room with another tourist from the group.

The group went whale watching the next day. Tom explained the behavior of the whales to Young. "Touch is very important to them. Whales and dolphins spend thirty percent of their time in physical contact with one another. They don't have hands, so they use other parts of their bodies to caress and investigate, and to carry things around. But they don't dream. Only humans do that. Dreaming is our privilege," Tom said.

"Maybe whales have different ways to dream. The way their minds work is a wonderful mystery to us. I love to dream and be mysterious. A romantic vision is hard to attain," Young said.

"I always dream. My dream has been answered. It is not in a distant place. It's here. I dreamed about traveling with you and it came true." Tom clasped her hands. She didn't resist.

As their stay on the Big Island approached the end, Young and Tom broke off from the group to be on their own. After dinner, they sat on the deck under the moonlight drinking wine. A gentle breeze softly touched their faces and the blazing torch lamps chased away the nighttime chill. Tom held her hands and said in a soft but confident voice, "Young, I think … I think I love you. It's just hard for me to say. I don't want to be alone any longer. Please stay with me. You give me more love than any other woman I've had in my life. You're like an angel to me. You came to me at just the right time. I am touched and moved by your grace. I am in love with you."

A radiant smile lit up her face. She buried her head into his chest and whispered, "I love you too, Tom. I had a dream and it came true tonight." Tom kissed Young and she sobbed with happiness.

The pair left the island the next day. They looked back at the island shimmering in the twilight haze. "We are going to miss this paradise," Young said. "It'll be just for a while, not for too long. We'll be back," Tom assured her. They glanced back again at the island. It seemed smaller and lonelier from a distance. So many memories were lingering in their minds.

After they returned from the trip, Tom and Young grew closer. Young visited his house frequently, cooking Korean food for him and washing and ironing his shirts. Tom was very happy. "You brought warmth to this house. It was such a wasteland. It feels like the last time I had laughter before you was the Stone Age. This place is full of happiness now and I appreciate you very much," Tom said. He explored the possibility of their marriage and Young didn't stop him.

"Tom, what are your plans for next Saturday?"

"I don't have any plans. It's just another day. Why are you asking? Do you want to go out to eat?"

"No, it's your birthday. Are you wondering how I know? I got it from your chart. It's strange. Nobody comes here to celebrate with you. I mean your son and daughter."

"I don't think Michael even remembers my birthday. Jamie called and sent me a present."

"That's not enough. I'll prepare dinner. You can invite your friends if you want to."

"I have nobody to invite. Just you and me. Let's have a nice dinner at a fancy restaurant. You don't have to cook. You've fed me enough. Look at my big belly." They both laughed. They had a memorable birthday dinner.

After Tom's birthday, Young suddenly disappeared. She didn't come to Sands Point, didn't respond to his emails, didn't answer his frequent calls, and cut all contact with him. Tom was nervous, unstable, and greatly worried. Tom realized that something unexpected had happened to her. He was panicked and bewildered. He couldn't sleep or eat. He visited her at the hospital during her working hours. It was raining hard. Young was surprised to see his drenched and wind-whipped face. He was undaunted and asked in an impatient voice, "What happened to you? Why are you avoiding me? Did I hurt you?" He asked all kinds of questions. Young sobbed and extended him a letter from a law office. Tom looked at the envelope. It was from his son's law firm. After reading it, he was furious. Michael had sent a cryptic, threatening letter to her. The letter said, "You are trying to steal my father's money. If you don't stay away from him, I'll report you to the authorities and prosecute you for grand larceny." It was beyond Tom's imagination. How could Michael accuse this innocent woman? Tom sincerely apologized to her and said, "You are not guilty at all. You did absolutely nothing wrong. You are an honest, compassionate, and remarkable woman. Tom is a jerk. I'll address the problem. Please forgive me. I am terribly sorry about all of this."

As soon as he got home, Tom flopped his tired body onto the couch. It was a sad day. He couldn't control his rage. He regained his composure and called Michael.

“Michael, you sent a nasty letter to the nurse.”

“Yes, I did it to protect you. She’s feigning kindness to get to you and you’ve fallen into her trap. All she wants is your money—millions of dollars. Actually, it’s not even your money. It’s Mom’s money. You got it when you got divorced. I won’t let her steal your money and run away. You’ll bitterly regret this once you realize it.”

“Michael, you’re a lawyer. How can you accuse an innocent person without any evidence?”

“She approached you as a visiting nurse and lured you on the Hawaii trip. If I don’t stop her now, you’ll fall further into her grasp. Then you’ll lose all of the money, I mean, Mom’s money.”

Tom almost lost his temper. “Michael, I never asked you to represent me. Please stop it. If not, I’ll get my own lawyer and fight against you.”

“No, I can’t. She is trying to extort your money. I’ll employ all available legal means to stop her.”

“Michael, you make me sick. You and your mother don’t have an ounce of human kindness. Young is full of compassion. She has a tender heart, and you have a stone heart. Don’t get involved in my business. It’s my life, not yours. You don’t have any right to destroy my life." He hung up. He called the housekeeper and warned her not to talk to Michael.

A confrontation with his only son drove Tom to despair. He felt sorry for Young, the most innocent and compassionate woman he'd ever met. His heart attack and Michael's nasty letter to Young were like a nightmare, a train of unexpected disasters. Fortunately, Young understood that this was true love and that Michael could not be a threat to their relationship. They restored their trust and returned to normal. Tom thought they had reached the point where they should formalize their relationship.

He invited Jamie to dinner with Young. Jamie was initially not thrilled to be invited to dinner. She had heard many bad things about Young from Michael. After she saw Young's elegant face and calm demeanor, she couldn't help but see how much her father loved her. Jamie had no reason not to embrace her. Jamie concluded that Young was the one who would keep her father healthy and provide genuine care for him for the rest of his life. Jamie told her father that if he decided to marry Young, she would come to the wedding wholeheartedly. Jamie called her brother and told him what she saw at dinner. Michael was very unhappy. He didn't agree that his father should get married to the woman he had blatantly accused of trying to steal his father's money. He called Tom and voiced his strong opposition to the anticipated wedding. Tom was angry and said in a calm but firm voice, "This is my decision. I am not expecting you to be nice to her. Just be civil to her and make her feel comfortable."

"It's your decision, of course, but I won't see her. Keep her away from me. I won't be at your wedding."

One month later, on a beautiful Saturday evening, Tom formally proposed to Young. She said in a shy, happy voice, "Yes, I will be your wife."

The long wait was over. At forty-three, Youngsook Lee was a bride and married to Tom Curtis. They became husband and wife. It was a small wedding; only about a hundred guests were invited. The wedding ceremony was solemn and brief, lasting only half an hour. A reception followed. The guests were overjoyed. They wished lots of luck and happiness for the newlyweds. Tom sank into deep thought. His first wife was a brilliant and tough woman. But she didn't have a heart. She was a thinking machine, a computer. His life with her had been a waste. Now Young was his beloved wife. He pledged to keep her as a jewel for the rest of his life. Young gazed at her husband with adoration, as if she could read his mind. Their hearts met. One heart, not separate. They departed for Hawaii for their real honeymoon.

Upon returning from their honeymoon, Young moved into the Sands Point house. Tom wanted to keep the housekeeper to help his wife, but Young insisted that she maintain their home her own way. There was another reason for this. She didn't want the housekeeper to look over her shoulder and talk to Michael and Jamie. Young cooked, and Tom really liked it. They rearranged the furniture and the house was born again. Tom continued to teach at Stony Brook and pleaded with Young not to work at the hospital any longer. "Young, we don't need your earnings. I have enough to support us. You can use your time to enrich yourself with literature and to play golf with me. We can play together at Sands Point Country Club. We pay a lot in dues. I would love to travel with you. We can go on a cruise to Alaska in the summer and explore the Amazon in the winter." They were the perfect couple and the envy of Tom's friends.

Summer came and they went on the Alaskan cruise. It was refreshing, and they discovered the last frontier. The northern lights were a wonder to behold—a marvel and a mystery. They talked about making another trip to Alaska to explore further north.

After they returned, Tom discovered something uncomfortable with his prostate. He didn't say anything to his wife and made an appointment with his primary physician. The doctor found something alarming and referred him to a specialist. He was diagnosed with prostate cancer. It had already spread to his vital organs. Panic, fear, and grief surged through him and he strengthened his resolve. He wouldn't lose control. He had Young.

Young sensed something was not normal and demanded to know what was wrong with him. Tom told her everything he knew. His face was pale from the strain. His condition deteriorated and his heart began to weaken. Young prayed, "Lord, please save his brilliant mind. He is an extraordinary, intuitive person. Please give me the chance to love him more. There's too little love in the world. Please don't throw it away. I shielded myself from men for fear of passing love. His love came to me late, but not too late. He and I deserve a lasting love. Lord, please save him and our love." She realized sorrow would never leave her alone. It was looming over her. She had never seen him this frightened before, much worse than when she had first seen him after his heart attack. She wanted to scream out in denial. She kept her hands wrapped tightly around his and said, "Tom, don't worry. You've survived before and you'll win another battle."

Tom had surgery. It took three hours. She was too familiar with the sights, sounds, and smells of the operating room. She was in panic and wanted to cry out. After the surgery, the doctor said that the surgery was successful. Young knew that a successful surgery did not necessarily mean survival. She was extremely nervous. Young did everything she could to save her beloved husband but it was to no avail. Tom passed away on a cold February evening, leaving his wife behind. Young was devastated. She had lost everything: her husband, her dreams, her love.

About three weeks after Tom was buried, his attorney sent a letter to Young to come visit his office. Tom's attorney, Tim Thompson, unveiled Tom's will. Tom bequeathed his Sands Point house and eighty percent of his assets to Young, twenty percent to Jamie, and left nothing for Michael. Tim Thompson estimated that Tom left about ten million dollars to his wife. Michael, who had never visited his father when he was dying, filed a civil suit against Young claiming half of his father's inheritance. The case was dismissed in court. Young established a charity foundation and donated all of her inheritance and the house. She moved back to her apartment and went back to St. Francis hospital. She continued to work with a warm, caring mind and was respected by her patients. She whispered to herself, "I'll be the same caring nurse, but never fall in love with another patient. Tom was the only man I truly loved. He is no longer in this world, but his heart remains in my heart. Our hearts met and will never be apart."

A Tale of Two Widows

New Year's Day, 2014

About a million revelers packed a windy and bitter-cold Times Square on New Year's Eve. Countless other people spent hours in front of the TV in anticipation of the countdown: Ten, nine … four, three, two, one. When the ball dropped and the clock struck midnight, folks kissed, cheered, and celebrated a brand new year in a blizzard of confetti. It was both crazy and beautiful.

It was a new year, a new month, and a new day, but

it was also much more than that. It was the chance for a new beginning. The routine practice of turning to a new page on our calendars offers little thrill. So we invent more momentous customs that help us live life to our highest hopes and aspirations. The New Year's holiday essentially offers us the occasion to make up for lost time. Cheers!

Sunny Kim spent the evening with her late husband's family in Flushing. She brought them a fruit basket and a bottle of white wine. Her former in-laws hold a traditional service for the dead each New Year's Eve. First, they honor their ancestors. Then, they pay special tribute to their beloved son Song-min Kim, Sunny's husband, who died in the World Trade Center attacks in 2001. The evening filled their hearts with sadness, and their eyes with tears. After the service, Sunny bowed in the customary Korean manner and gave them some money. She returned home with a heavy heart in the dark and lonely early morning hours.

Snow fell that night. By sunrise, the earth was blanketed in five inches of white snow. It was a busy day for Sunny Kim. She woke up at about six in the morning and prepared rice cake soup while her husband and son slept in. After a late breakfast, she took the Long Island Rail Road to Penn Station and headed to downtown Manhattan. Her husband didn't ask her where she was going. He and her five-year-old son knew. It had become an annual tradition since that unforgettable day.

The wind blew as sharp as a knife off the Hudson under a dark and cloudy sky. Sunny tightened her scarf and buttoned her overcoat to brace herself for the journey to lower Manhattan. Hordes of people filled the streets, speaking languages from all over the world: German, French, Spanish, Chinese, and Japanese, among others. Occasionally, Sunny heard the familiar words of Korean. Christmas lights sparkled high on the trees and holiday music floated out of the shops. Sidewalk vendors sold hats, gloves, and gift items. Amid the bustle, tourists lined up to enter the 9/11 Memorial Park, located in the space where the World Trade Center towers once stood. The hours were extended for the New Year's holiday crowd. Sunny, numb from grief and winter's cold, entered a nearby gift shop to warm up; it was the sort of place where site-seers purchased 9/11 T-shirts, caps, books, and other gifts. A video recording played and replayed the sad stories of that tragic day on a TV monitor.

Sunny didn't linger. She trekked on into the park, passed the South Pool, and headed directly to the North Pool. In summer, the waterfall's mist offered reprieve from the day's heat. This time of the year, it added a frosty bite to the air. Flowers, more abundant than usual, adorned the site. Sunny stood in front of her husband's name, inscribed in bronze. His spirit had been there permanently since the park was established. Sunny placed a flower on the name panel and whispered to him: "Honey, I am back. How have you been? You must be cold. I went to your parents' house last night. They are getting old, but they look fine. We thought about you. It's been already more than twelve years. As I told you, I married again. Sorry, Honey. Please understand. You were my husband and you are still in my heart." She cried and touched his name over and over again. She felt he was looking at her with his caring eyes. She listened for his words, but heard nothing. A gentle breeze carried his only message: I love you, Sunny.

She looked around the park. The Freedom Tower stretched high into the sky. It was a magnificent building. The museum, a sign stated, would open in March. Hurricane Sandy had delayed its opening, she overheard a police officer say. Oak trees shivered in the frigid air. Just as Sunny turned to the gate to head home, somebody called her name.

"Sunny, how are you? It's been so long. It's like you're a stranger."

At first, she didn't recognize who was speaking. Then she saw a woman wrapped in a fur coat wearing tall boots, walking with a man and her son.

"Oh, Judy, you look great. Who is this young man? Is this your boy?"

"It's been twelve years. Even rivers and mountains change, as Koreans say. By the way, this is my husband, Tom. We've been married for ten years. We have a girl. She didn't come with us. And you know my son, James. He is a college student now. He is studying business at NYU."

Her husband extended his hand and greeted her, "Nice to meet you." He was a handsome white man in his forties. He looked intelligent and carried a natural charm. “I was born and schooled here in Westchester. My high school friend is here. He worked for Cantor Fitzgerald. He was very smart. He got his MBA from Walton. It was sad to lose him,” he said.

“Did you go to his panel?” Sunny asked.

“Yeah, briefly. You know, it happened twelve years ago. We can’t bear it forever.” Judy said.

“But I still feel very sad. He is in my heart. Even though I remarried.”

“Oh, you did. Congratulations! You should have invited me.”

“It was a small wedding. We got married at church with only family and close friends as witnesses. We had a reception at the church.”

Tom looked away, seemingly disinterested in the conversation.

“Sunny, are you busy this evening?” asked Judy. “If not, let’s have dinner together. We live in California, and are heading home tomorrow. We planned to shop this afternoon. Tom wants to buy a coat at Brooks Brothers.” They agreed to meet at 6 p.m. in K-town, the Korean part of midtown Manhattan, then parted ways.

Tuesday, September 11, 2001

On a perfectly beautiful September day, not a cloud in the sky, Song-min Kim, like millions of men and women, got ready for work. He boarded the 7 train from Flushing and transferred to the R at Times Square to get to Wall Street. He got off at the Twin Towers and rode the elevator up to his office at the Internal Revenue Service, where he was always the first to arrive. He put his lunch of sandwich and water in the office fridge. It was 8:20 a.m.

Sunny was a clothing designer for a fairly big apparel manufacturer on 7th Avenue that made women's skirts, tops, and high-end jeans. About two hundred people worked there. Sunny designed mostly blouses. She joined the company after graduating from New York's Fashion Institute of Technology, or FIT, about five years earlier. Her fashion acumen was sharp, and her manager noticed her talent immediately. She was assigned many important projects and was an indispensable member of the design team.

Sunny woke up that morning feeling uneasy. A nightmare the night before had frightened her. In her dreams, a fishing boat capsized out in the ocean with her husband aboard. He desperately called out to her for help. She woke up sweating in the dead of night, relieved to find that her husband was fast asleep next to her. She touched his warm hands and kissed him lightly. When they parted at the train station that morning, she told him to be careful, and to take care. "Give me a ring at lunch time. I packed a tuna sandwich for you."

At 9 a.m. Sunny turned on her computer to start drawing when a co-worker rushed into the office screaming, "Oh my gosh! Something really terrible is happening at the World Trade Center! Turn on the TV!" Sunny couldn't believe what she was hearing. "What? Where? What happened? Are you serious or joking?"

"Find a TV. The World Trade Center is on fire!" the co-worker demanded.

"What? The Twin Towers? My husband is there. Oh my God." They rushed to the manager's office and turned on the TV.

As Sunny realized what was going on, she screamed and ran out of the office in a panic with the intention of heading downtown. But the trains were all stopped. Sunny ran down 7th Avenue, walking only when she needed to catch her breath. She could think only of getting to the Towers. She was dazed, and not in her right mind. Then she saw it. The Towers were ablaze.

"Oh my God! Oh, my God. Song-min, are you okay? Get out of the building quickly. Jump out of the widow if you can. No, no, no. Don't jump. It's too high. God, please save him. Oh, please. He is a good man." She cried. She was not able to go any farther. When she reached 14th Street, the police stopped all traffic. She pleaded, "My husband is there. Let me go."

The man looked at her sadly. "Lady, I understand, but you can't go. Please go back to where you were. Go to a safe place."

She couldn't say anything. All she could do was cry. Suddenly she thought about her father-in-law and mother-in-law. They were at their dry cleaning store on Long Island. She tried to call them, but there was no cell service. She rushed to a pay phone. No signal.

"Oh, God! Now they will really resent me," she said out loud to herself. She walked north aimlessly. When she returned to her office, the entrance was closed.

A guard asked about her well-being and said, "Why are you wandering around here? Everybody's left. People say the Empire State Building is next. Get out of the city quickly." "What happened to the World Trade Center?"she asked. Her head was foggy.

He looked at her with an alarmed face and answered, "Did you come from outer space? The towers collapsed. Thousands of people died."

She had to believe it now. There was little hope of her husband's survival.

Sunny walked north toward the 59th Street Bridge. It was a refugee march. Everybody walked north to escape the danger looming in southern Manhattan. People didn't talk much; they just walked, or ran. They were experiencing something they had never imagined. How could this happen in New York? In this country? She crossed the bridge at about 6 p.m. On the other side, she noticed people waiting to use phone booths. She stood in line for about ten minutes before she was able to place the call to her husband's parents at home. Her mother-in-law answered.

"Mother, it's me. Have you heard?" They didn't say much. All they could do was sob. Finally, Sunny said, "Mother, I will be home soon." Sunny lived at the same two-family house with her in-laws in Flushing, near Kissena Park. She hailed a cab and arrived home one hour later.

Sunny's husband never came home. Sick with grief, Sunny could not eat at all, but she cooked dinner for her in-laws, as she always did. They didn't touch their food. They didn't talk much. All they could do was watch TV and hope for a miracle. They nervously watched the door and eagerly grabbed the phone when it rang, weeping all the while. After three days passed in silence, Sunny's in-laws went to their store. They couldn't leave it closed forever. Sunny stayed home. Her boss told her to take her time and return to work only after she was able to settle down.

The days after 9/11 were an extension of the disaster that changed the whole world. The bright autumn sun rose every morning, as if nothing had happened. It was partly fear and partly illness that clouded her judgment. Every day was torture. Sunny couldn't look at her in-laws. It was not her fault, but somehow she felt guilty. Why did this happen to us? She was trapped in her room. She couldn't eat, talk, or even concentrate on anything. She tried to comfort her in-laws. They turned their backs. They were unwilling to look at her. They lived in the same house, but in separate worlds.

Sunny's own parents worried about her a lot. They wanted her to move back in with them, but she declined. She chose to stay with her in-laws, even though she was uncomfortable. She visited her parents when her in-laws went to work, but she always came back to prepare their dinner. Her parents loved Sunny's husband. He had been good to them, and treated them like his own parents.

Weeks passed. Not a single day went by without thinking of him. The whole thing seemed like a nightmare. Sunny came to realize that it was not a dream, just the cold truth, a reality she had to face. Her relationship with her in-laws was strained. They completely ignored her, refusing to talk to her. She overheard them whispering.

"She brought a disaster to us," her father-in-law

said. "She was an omen. My son died because he married her."

Sunny was stunned. She protested, "Do you know how much I loved him? Don't you see that he really loved me? Everybody said we were lovebirds. We were a happy, newly married couple."

Her mother-in-law suggested that she move back in with her own parents. She was banished. They kicked her out. She cried and reluctantly moved out.

Sunny sensed that her husband's parents were not happy with their son's choice of a wife. They never came right out and said it, but she knew they despised her family. Sunny's family had emigrated to Argentina in the 1980's. Her parents were uneducated and poor. They had a clothing store in Seoul. Business was bad; they barely made a living. Her uncle lived in Sao Paulo and owned a garment business. Sunny's family tried to move there, but couldn't get an immigration visa. Argentina's immigration laws were a bit easier. So they moved to Argentina first, instead of Brazil, and opened a ladies apparel shop. Sunny was ten years old then. She helped her parents and learned about fashion.

After living there for five years, they decided to move to the United States. It was not easy, but they managed to find a way. They couldn't speak English or Spanish, but they knew how to swim upstream in the world. They settled in Flushing and opened a fish market. Sunny started her schooling at Frances Lewis High School. She studied English as a second language and worked really hard, eventually graduating with honors. She was accepted at FIT. Being a famous fashion designer was her dream. Sunny met Judy there, whose Korean name was Joo-hee. Judy had come from Korea with a student visa. She was one of the best dressed Korean students. She was pretty and wore very expensive designer jackets, pants, and shoes. Other students whispered that Judy was a surgically carved beauty. Her face changed every time she came back from Korea. She dated a white guy at NYU. She often changed partners. Judy liked Sunny, even though she was two years younger. They liked to go to K-town together to eat Korean food.

Sunny met Song-min Lee at a Korean church. They were members of the college mission team.

Song-min studied accounting at NYU. He was a quiet but confident man. They started dating. Song-min's parents were not particularly happy with their close relationship from the very start. Sunny heard indirectly that they regarded Sunny's family as low class. They were not pleased about her parents' birthplace. They were born and raised in the southwestern part of Korea. Song-min's family was from a more prominent area in the southeastern section of Korea. His parents worked jobs they didn't like, but they were college educated, a distinction that they held in high regard. They were parochial and old-fashioned people who were not ready to adapt to a fast-changing social environment. When Sunny packed her belongings, they avoided looking at her. She became a total outcast after their son perished.

10 p.m., September 11, 2001, Seoul

Judy celebrated her father's sixtieth birthday with

a lavish family dinner for fifty people at a hotel in downtown Seoul. Her father's family and cousins, her mother's family, and her father's close friends attended. They drank expensive wine and cut a big birthday cake. Judy was one of three children, and the only girl. Her older brother worked for LG, and her younger brother was a graduate student majoring in finance. She took a two-week vacation to attend her father's birthday party. She acquired her permanent U.S. residency card three years after her marriage to Hyung-man Kang. The couple had one child, a lovely boy, now five years old. Judy introduced him to many of his Korean relatives for the first time.

When they returned home, Judy's mother turned on the TV to watch the news. The news anchor stumbled, hesitated for a few minutes, and announced that he had breaking news. The World Trade Center was on fire. Unbelievable images appeared on the TV screen. Judy's mother called her daughter in.

"Joo-hee, look at this. Something bad has happened in New York. Passenger planes were hijacked, and the World Trade Center is burning." Judy was stunned. She watched the news, thinking about her husband.

He was working in the South Tower.

"Mom, my husband is there," she screamed. "He works on the eighty-seventh floor. He is in danger. Oh my God! Oh my God!"

The whole family watched the news restlessly all night. Judy called her husband's parents in New York. No answer. All planes were grounded, telephone service was out, and the whole country was in a state of emergency. Judy cried with her sleepy son. She thought about her husband's decision to stay behind in New York. He said he wanted to go with her, but couldn't leave his work.

Judy called Korean Air the next day. They said they didn't know when they could fly again. When she told them her husband was in the World Trade Center, they expressed sympathy and promised she would be the first passenger to be notified. They called her the next day with flight information. They said that JFK airport was closed but West Coast airports would soon be open. She booked a flight to LA with the intention of transferring to a domestic flight to New York. Judy finally arrived in New York one week after the disaster. She tried to get in touch with her husband's parents. Nobody answered. They thought she was in Seoul. She went to their apartment. It was deadly quiet; her beloved husband was nowhere to be seen. It was like a ghost house. Sadness filled their sweet home. No laughter, no music, no food—nothing. In a week, she had lost everything. She looked at their wedding picture. Her thoughts drifted back to her husband's parents. They lived in Corona, Queens. She went there with her son. When she knocked on the front door, there was no answer. She figured they went to church. She left a note: "I am back from Korea. I watched the news on TV. I am praying he is alive. I will come back tomorrow afternoon. Please take care of yourself."

She visited them the next day. As soon as they saw her, they wept. "It was like thunder from out of the blue," her mother-in-law said. "Beyond imagination. That day changed everything. We couldn't sleep, eat, or think. We were in total shock. We still cannot believe what has happened. Every day we are waiting for him. Whenever we hear cars pass by, we look outside. He was your husband and also our son." They wept, holding each other.

Judy met her husband after she graduated from FIT. He was not particularly to her liking at first. She liked energetic, outgoing, charming guys. He was quite the opposite: a tacit, shy, and unsocial man. He wasn't a sharp dresser. He always wore jeans and a sweatshirt. Even when they went to parties, he didn't look his best. Judy eventually bought him a fine jacket and pants to wear to help enhance his good looks, and to save her own face. But he was brilliant. He graduated from Bronx Science and was accepted into Columbia University. His parents wanted him to be a medical doctor, but he liked math and computer science. He was a computer genius. He received a dual master's degree in math and computer science. He was scouted by a big investment company and worked in the IT department. Judy proudly displayed his Columbia degree on the most visible wall in their apartment. She liked his Ivy League degree more than he did. Judy's parents were exceedingly proud of him. They knew he was not a PhD, but still often boasted to their friends: "Our son-in-law is a Columbia doctor." Judy's husband wanted to live with his parents, but Judy strongly protested. They rented a two-bedroom apartment near the Brooklyn Museum. She seldom visited her in-laws—only on special occasions, like his parents' birthdays, Thanksgiving, and New Year's Day.

New Year's Day, 2014

Sunny and Judy met that night at 6 p.m. at their favorite restaurant in K-town. New York's K-town is the home of Koreans, who come from all over the place to visit here. There are many restaurants, karaoke bars, bakeries, hotels, and gift shops here. There's even an old Korean book store. As soon as people enter 32nd Street, they smell all sorts of Korean food. Korean students on the east coast love to visit; it's their home sweet home. It had been so long since Sunny and Judy had spent time together in this familiar place. They ordered their favorite dishes: Judy, a barbecue beef; Sunny, a Jeonju *bibimbap.* They ordered two glasses of red wine. Sunny only sipped a little of her wine. Judy drank the full glass.

"Did you go home after I saw you this morning, or did you wander around here?" Sunny asked.

"We went to Brooks Brothers. Tom got a winter coat, and my son bought a jacket. It's an expensive store, but they like it. Where did you go, Sunny?"

"Oh, I had some time, so I went to Century 21. I got my husband a warm jacket, and boots for my son. They were inexpensive. There is a Century 21 not far from where I live, but this store has a better selection. I called my husband to tell him that I am not eating at home tonight. I prepared rice cake soup and barbecue ribs this morning."

"When did you get married? What is he doing these days?"

"I got married five years after 9/11. I thought about staying unmarried, but people pushed me to get a new life. I felt guilty marrying again. My husband knew him. We were in the same group at our church. After that tragedy, he comforted me for a long time. He was not married and asked me to be his wife. I was lonely and I was sure he loved me. He wholeheartedly embraced me. He is an engineer and a very good man.

We have a son. He's five years old now."

"That's good. Why did you feel bad about your remarriage? It's not your fault. What happened was what happened. It's your life. Of course you should remarry and start a new life. You can't cry forever."

"I know, but still ..."

"Still what? I got remarried two years after 9/11. Of course I was in pain for a while. But I am not the kind of woman to keep crying in my room. I tried to forget him after a few months. After I got the compensation money, I left New York and moved to San Diego. I didn't want to face his family. Why should I? They were important to me when their son was my husband. Once he was gone, they were nothing to me.

I met Tom in San Diego, we dated about a year, and got married in 2003. It was his second and my second, too. Of course, my case was unique. He is a caring, nice man. He is an investment banker. He didn't touch my compensation fund, but I chipped in one million dollars for our new home. It's a pretty big house. You can stay at our place whenever you come to visit us. Especially during the cold months. I reserved the rest of the fund for my son's education.

We bought an apartment in SoHo for him. I didn't want him to come to New York, but he likes it here. I guess he still remembers his father and wants to stay close to him. He visits the memorial park occasionally and leaves flowers for him. He is his natural father's son, not my present husband's boy. That's perfectly okay to me."

"Judy, my in-laws blamed their son's death on me. They were superstitious. They thought I brought bad luck to them. They kicked me out after he died."

"Really? That's ridiculous. You didn't have to stay with them anyway. If I were you, I would say thank you and never see them again. Never."

"Actually I felt terribly sorry for them. I had a bad dream the night before. If I'd stopped him from going to work, he would still be alive." Sunny wept.

"You are a weak-minded woman. Nothing you could do under the circumstances. They were bad. You should cut all ties with them."

"I still see them. At least twice a year. On New Year's Eve and his birthday."

"You didn't give them any money, did you?"

"What money?"

"The compensation money from the memorial fund."

Sunny hesitated.

"You shared it. You're stupid. Why did you? It was your money. You were the sole beneficiary."

"Judy, it was very difficult. I thought a lot about it, talked to my friends, sought advice from a counselor. Money is important, but ..."

"But what? They didn't deserve it. They chased you out like a stray dog."

"He was their son. His mother gave birth, they raised him, they educated him. He had been their beloved son all his lifetime. I happened to marry him and lived with him for two years. Now he's gone. He is still their son. He was buried in their hearts."

"So how much did you give them?"

Sunny was uncomfortable talking about money. She had felt like dividing her late husband's death money. "I gave them half," she said. "I can live without that money. My parents agreed with me. I bought a house with that money after I remarried."

"You are very generous, if not stupid. I didn't give any to his parents. I kept everything and moved to California. They were good people. They didn't ask for any. Of course they wanted some, I guessed. I disregarded the idea. If I gave them a little, they would not be happy. I was his wife. He had life insurance. I got a good compensation check from his company, too. All together it was about four million dollars. Later on, his church sent me a letter. His parents wanted to build a mission center in Honduras in his name. I sent 200,000 dollars to the church. That was it. No more. And I have had virtually no contact with his parents since. One day they came to San Diego and called me to see their grandson. I didn't go out. Why did they come without telling me a word?"

"How could you do that, Judy? I think you went too far. You were cruel to them. I still think Song-min's parents are my in-laws. And they treated me better after I gave them the money. I never imagined I could have that much in my life. It was unanticipated money."

"Well, money is money. Actually, it was pure money because it had been donated by so many good hearts."

"It was sad money. Whenever I touch that fund my heart aches. I see his smiling face, and think about the happy moments we shared."

"Sunny, don't be too sentimental. It's been twelve years. We were young then. We are in our forties now. Look forward. Not backward. The past is the past. The present is important. Your dead husband cannot feed you. You have to feed yourself and your family. The dead cannot make you happy. He only makes you sad. Those happy days are gone, never to return. You have to rebuild your life."

"Judy, you are realistic. I am not. I still live with the memory. Sadness is an important part of my life. It makes me humble, sincere, and deep."

"Don't look at the Towers. Look over the Towers. There is bright sunshine there. Birds are flying. It's so beautiful. No sorrow there. Peace and happiness."

"Whenever I look at the Towers, I feel sad. You saw sunshine over the Towers; I saw dark clouds. One time I was soaked with rain in the memorial park. His ashes stuck to my blouse. I didn't wash it. He is still in my heart."

The two women said goodbye. One smiled. One cried. It was dark. Flurries fell. Sunny looked at the Freedom Tower. She said, "Goodbye, Honey. Have a happy New Year!"

The Mountain Rats

"Look at that house," I said to my wife. "Do you think somebody lives there, or is it abandoned?"

"I have no idea," she said. "We can take a look."

The house was positioned at the edge of a pond. It looked okay from a distance. But as we slowly approached, the place looked haunted. It was overgrown with weeds. The glass in all the windows was missing, most of the roof shingles had blown off, and vines hung from badly deteriorated gutters. The birds were singing as we got out of the car and walked closer. Chipmunks and squirrels chased after each other. That was the only sign of life. The house belonged to the birds and wild animals. Nature owned the place.

We didn't go to the Catskills looking for old houses. We were on our way home after three days of golfing at Hanna Country Club. We were in Delaware County, which is about a two-and-a-half-hour drive north of New York City. Our golf club members had gone there every September. We usually arrived on a Thursday morning and played a round of golf. We'd play thirty-six holes on Friday and Saturday. On Sunday, we'd get an early start to enjoy the morning, and then head home around 1 or 2 p.m. That particular day was beautiful: cloudless, breezy, and warm. We were driving along Route 28 South when we spotted a run-down house next to a small pond. The two-story house stood alone, not far from the road, just a few miles from a village. There were no other houses around. I don't know why, but I took a picture of the house before heading back home.

We first went to the Catskills about thirty-five years ago. We lived in Washington Heights, Manhattan.

We had a small retail store at the time. One Sunday, around Mother's Day, we went on a picnic. Without a clear destination, our family just climbed in the car and drove north to the mountains. We had two kids then, Erin and Susan. My mother-in-law, who was living with us, had joined us for the ride. Our third daughter Stacey was not yet born. The weather was nice but a little chilly. When we reached the foothills of the mountain, my wife complained of being carsick, so we stopped alongside a stream to take a break and eat lunch. Suddenly, my mother-in-law shouted something.

"Come here! There are so many fiddleheads here."

"What, Mom? Fiddleheads?"

"Yes, plenty of them. And they are good—fat and big. I'll pick all of them."

My wife joined her, and she was really surprised. The fiddleheads were top quality. Americans don't know anything about this plant, but Koreans love it. We picked baskets of them that day. Afterwards, we hiked to the top of the mountain and found a beautiful park. We enjoyed the day. At the time, we had lived in New York for only a few years. We had no idea where we were, and didn't even know the name of the town. Looking back, I only remember that we had been somewhere in the heart of the Catskills. The following spring we tried to return to that same spot to pick fiddleheads, but we couldn't find the stream. We had forgotten about that area, deep in the Catskill Mountains, until we started playing golf at Hanna Golf Course.

My name is Boklim Choi. I am a first-generation Korean immigrant. Americans call me Peter. Boklim was the name given by my father, whether I liked it or not. I knew it sounded strange and was hard to pronounce, but Boklim is my name. When I started my first business, my American friend said to me, "You need to have an easy name like John, David, Mark, or Peter." I hesitated. He pushed me, and started calling me Peter. Soon all my non-Korean friends were calling me Peter.

In Korea, I was a journalist. But my knowledge and experience there were of no use here in America. In New York I have spent almost twenty years working as an ethnic newspaper reporter and editor, and also as a Korean cable TV news analyst. I've published two poetry books, a golf essay collection, and two novels, all in Korean. I still contribute essays to a Korean newspaper. Korean-Americans here know me as a journalist.

I'm kind of retired now from my golf retail business. I work for a few hours three days a week, as well as Sundays. I was never an athletic person. I am not generally fond of sports, but I like golf and baseball. I'm a Yankees fan. I haven't gone to Yankee stadium much, only a few times. I watch the games on TV. Golf is my favorite sport. My handicap is high; I seldom score in the low nineties, sometimes over a hundred on a challenging course. Oh, I love to bet; without betting I have no fun. I am almost always the loser when I bet.

I used to go to the Grossinger, Concord, and Swan Lake golf courses with friends many years ago, but not anymore. Somehow as I grew older, I lost my passion for golf. Golf consumes too much time and it's expensive. You need a whole day to play, and it costs me about one hundred dollars each time. I am using my time and money now for other purposes.

I live in Port Washington, NY. I love that town; it's

the best home I've ever had. I live in a townhouse right along Harbor Links Golf Course. It has a gym, swimming pool, and community center, and the beach is only a few minutes away. I always walk to the beach, even on rainy days. Occasionally, I walk in the winter. My house is a good size—not big, but spacious enough to have my own bed and study. I spend a good deal of my time every day reading and writing. I write in both English and Korean. Of course, my Korean is much better than my English.

I have traveled extensively. I have been to Alaska and to the Amazon. I crossed Siberia by train in the 1980s before the Berlin Wall was crumpled. Along the way, I've seen many different ways of life, and many abandoned houses. I've always wondered why people live in fifty-below weather in Alaska, or in a place where temperatures rise above ninety degrees in the Amazon. It's just beyond my imagination how people withstand such conditions. What amazed me the most was that the people in such places looked comfortable, happy. They were relaxed, just taking in whatever nature delivered.

One of my favorite books is Daniel Defoe's *Robinson*

Crusoe. I became fascinated with Crusoe and how he overcame all adversity. After seeing that dilapidated mountain house, I started thinking about Crusoe, and how he built his house and raised animals and grew fruit to survive. No matter what I would need to endure in the Catskills, I thought, I could manage and fare far better than poor, desperate Crusoe. No comparison. Crusoe was shipwrecked. He battled a mighty storm, and was thrown alone, by the sea onto an uninhabited island. Crusoe was miserable and helpless. I am not. Certainly, I could survive and make a life for myself in the Catskill Mountains. I would be only miles away from civilization. Most importantly, I would have the companionship of my family. Now, I have the sense to know that I am neither brave nor strong enough to face the challenges Crusoe had met. But Crusoe lived in a different time, I reasoned. Once I saw that abandoned house in the Catskills, I yearned to live deep in the mountains, away from all the conveniences of modern life. But I couldn't share my stupid thoughts with my wife. She would say, "Are you crazy? Go there and live by yourself."

I drove back to the mountains a few weeks later to take another look at that desolate house without saying a word to my wife. I drove down Route 28 West and stopped at a rest area. There was a tourist information center, a little eatery, and a shopping center. I bought a few items and chatted with the cashier.

"I saw some abandoned houses around here. Are there many?"

"Sure. All over the Town of Shandaken."

"If I want to take a look, what should I do?

"Go to the town office. They will give you the history of the house and some information. But why? Do you want to buy one?"

"No, I am just curious. My wife would kill me if I bought an abandoned place."

"I would kill my husband if he tried that," the cashier said.

"So, where is the town office?"

"It's only five to six minutes from here. Just head west."

A man in his fifties had listened in on our conversation. He let me know that I could get a lot more information in the Ulster County Offices. But first, I felt compelled to get a closer look at that property, just a few miles away. I parked my car alongside the local road, got out of the car, and walked around the pond, where two swans were swimming. It was late autumn, and the water's surface reflected the clear blue sky. No doubt, I thought, there were fish in that pond. I heard the whisper of a stream, and walked west to find a cool current of water flowing alongside the pond. It was bigger than the one I saw at Hanna Golf Course, about half the size of the Jordan River. The water was not deep, but clear and ice-cold. Its music felt to me like a message from the ancient Catskills. The house stood on the plain of a steep hill that must have been a small foot of the Adirondack Mountain. As I walked toward the old white house, I had a strange feeling. What if somebody sees me? He might think I was insane or homeless looking for a night's sleep. I was excited, but also fearful. The owner of the house might bring out a rifle and shoot me.

"Hello, is anybody in this house?" I yelled. No answer. Just as I had expected. I waited a few minutes and yelled again. I heard only the breeze whistle. There was a wooden fence around the house, and a gate with no latch. I opened the gate and cautiously entered. A frightened squirrel darted off. It scared me. Among the overgrown weeds in the front yard stood two big trees. In the backyard, there was another tall tree that shaded a good part of the house. The old slate patio was badly fractured. The rotten wooden railings were ready to give way. I wanted to look at the interior of the house. But, again, I felt uneasy. I yelled, "Hello, anybody here?"

I entered through the back door, which was unlocked. Singing birds filled the home's interior. There were bird nests, with baby birds nestled in one of them. The mother bird watched me, ready to attack at any moment. I was clearly an intruder, and an enemy to watch. The place was crawling with ants. It was a house for birds and ants. Every living thing ought to have a place to sleep, I realized, even the animals. They need shelter, just as we do. I continued my self-guided tour. The house had a decent-sized living room, a workroom, a bedroom, and a full-sized bathroom, and a kitchen with a small pantry on the main floor. There was a fireplace and a rusty old stove. The wood floor was cracking. There was no basement. After peeking around, I went upstairs. There were two bedrooms, another living room, and a small bathroom with no bathtub. Since much of the roof was missing, watermarks stained every surface. The place smelled rotten. The house was dying, if not dead. It was abandoned long ago, and neglected. I felt sorry for it. I thought the house had the wrong owner. It was a crisp, chilly November day. A gust of fresh air filled the deserted house. The brilliant sunshine was abundant. As soon as I left the house, it once again belonged to nature.

I visited the assessor's office of the town of Shandaken the next day. It was a two-story building, much smaller than I had expected. About ten cars filled the parking lot. I had called the office the preceding day, so I knew whom to talk to. I looked for Sherry. She was a mid-aged woman, maybe in her early fifties.

"Which house are you interested in? Do you have the address?" she asked.

"No I don't. It is close to a pond about two miles

north of the Emerson Information Center."

"I don't know exactly which one. I'll show you a picture. Is it this one?"

I looked at it carefully and said, "Yes, that's the one. How old is this house?"

"Let's see. It was built in 1890, so a hundred and thirteen years old. The original builder was Mr. Tom Sullivan." She studied the history of the house, then said, "It never changed ownership."

"How long has the house been abandoned?" I asked.

"They haven't paid property taxes since 2005. Ulster County seized it in 2008. Now it's county property. They hadn't paid taxes for three years. Did you look at the place?"

"Yes, I did. It looked fantastic, and awful. It looked fantastic because it was standing by a pond, and awful because it's in such disrepair."

"How do you know that? Did you enter the house?"

"Yes, I peeked from the outside and inside."

"You shouldn't enter that place without permission. It's county property."

"I am so sorry. It was too tempting. I apologize."

"That's okay. I won't report it. By the way, what

makes you so interested in that house? Do you want to buy it?"

"I don't know yet. I might. I have to talk to my wife. She is my boss."

"I would always listen to my wife. Husbands should always listen to their wives." Sherry laughed. "If you want to acquire the house, you have to bid in an auction and win it."

She gave me the address and contact number of the Ulster County office. "I want you to be careful," she said. "The area was severely flooded many years ago. Virtually the whole town was under water, and people died. The house might have been flooded for at least two to three weeks. Take another look, and then decide. I don't want you to make a mistake."

She gave me her business card. "If anybody asks you," she said, "show this card." She seemed uneasy of my keen interest in the place.

I headed back to the place again and studied the exterior and the surrounding area. An old man was fishing at the pond. He spotted me from the distance and yelled. "Who's that? Why are you here?" I approached him. "I am not a thief or an arsonist,"

I said. "The town sent me to look at this house." I showed him the business card.

"I know her. She is a fixture over there. She's been there for at least twenty years. I visited the office to reduce my property tax." He looked at me carefully and said, "안녕하십니까?" (How are you?). I was surprised and responded, "안녕하십니까? Where did you learn Korean?"

"I was in the Korean War. I fought in Dongducheon and Inje. I was injured, almost lost one of my legs." He showed me a big scar on his left leg. "I was brought to a field hospital and stayed there about three months, was discharged, and fought again."

"Thanks for your great service. You saved our country. I truly appreciate your fight for freedom."

"I was only a small part of the American army. I was twenty years old then. We had three Korean War vets here in this county. Two are gone, and one left. That's me." The expression on his face changed, and he asked, "Why did you peek into the Sullivan's house? They've been gone for a long while."

"Since 2005, they said. They didn't pay their taxes."

"The Sullivans were good people. They were Scots.

The first generation, Tom Sullivan, came from the Highlands in Scotland. That is a very cold, windy, deserted part in Scotland. His son, Eddie, was my friend. He was five years my senior. We skied, hunted, fished, and played golf together. He was a good golfer, a long driver with an excellent short game. I always lost money to him. He went to the Second World War. After he returned from the war, he worked for the county government. He died of a heart attack at the age of seventy. He is remembered as a warm and caring man in this town."

"I'm very sorry. Sometimes good guys leave first, unfortunately," I said.

"Oh, my name is Harry Reed. My father came from Northern Ireland. People crossed the channel with a small boat or with a canoe. It's very close. Scotland and Northern Ireland have mantained a good relationship. They both hated England. Now they are part of the UK. History is ironic. As time changes, everything changes."

"Where do you live? Is it far from here?"

"Not far. About 10 minutes on foot. If you move in I'll be your closest neighbor. Are you considering buying the house? The view is good, but it's so decayed. You have to think twice. It needs hundreds of thousands of dollars for renovation and it doesn't pay."

"When was the last time you saw Sullivan?"

"Several years ago. A violent tropical storm hit this town. Bridges collapsed, villages washed away, and numerous houses were flooded. Many places never recovered. Eddie's son Ken Sullivan owned the place. His own house was under water from two days of torrential rain. I've never seen such a storm in my life. My house was partially destroyed too. The local sheriff rescued many people. It was the worst disaster in the Catskills. Then one day, he packed up and disappeared."

"Have you seen him since, and do you know where he went? Does he have a family?"

"Ken had a wife and two kids, a boy and a girl. Oh, they were lovely. He came to see me before he left. He had an uncle in New York City, and moved there temporarily. Later on I heard he was working for the federal government, in the Department of Homeland Security as a security officer. His job is to locate hidden drugs and bombs. He works with dogs. The dogs sniff out bombs and controlled substances. A dog is his boss; without it he cannot get paid."

It was getting dark. I looked at his fishing bucket. No fish. He said it was okay. He said he could still enjoy a drink and dinner. I asked him if it was okay with him if I bought him dinner. He agreed. Before we left the pond I suggested to him that we take a look at the house one more time. At the house, a herd of deer had wandered down from the mountain and were grazing and nosing around in the backyard. Surprisingly, the deer were not frightened. We heard birds singing inside the house.

"You know, it's their house now," Harry said. "When people move out, animals move in. Sure it is. It's their place until somebody moves in. We are the strangers. This mountain is their home."

Our talk continued over drinks and dinner. We each had a few glasses of beer. I had a lot of questions. "Were you born in the Catskills? Do you like it here?"

"I am a mountain rat. I was born and raised here and never left. I will die here. I am eighty-one years old. I am getting old with this mountain. The whole

Catskills are my home."

"So you know everybody here. If I moved here, would you help me until I got settled?"

"Of course I would. I love Koreans. My doctor is Korean. I drive to Kingston every three months to see him. I have high blood pressure and a heart problem. Thank God, I am still breathing. He is taking good care of me. And I like kimchi. It's spicy, but I like garlic. I don't have a family here. My wife died years ago, and my kids moved out of the Catskills long ago as well. They hate this mountain. But I love it."

"I am starting to love the mountain, too. I cannot be a mountain rat like you, but I think I can enjoy the tranquil country life."

"People cannot leave here because of the mountain's magical embrace. It's only a hundred miles away from the biggest city on the planet, but it's a different world. Once it gets into your blood, you cannot leave here. You become a mountain rat. The Catskills have become such a rich legacy for many people."

"I saw some Jewish people here. When did they start to move here?"

"About a hundred years ago. The Catskills shaped

American Jewish culture, enabling them to become Americans. Locals liked the German Jews more than the East-European Jews. We can still feel the presence of Jewish culture here. There are lots of them in Ulster and Sullivan Country.

"Did locals embrace the Jews?"

"Not at first. But they liked their money. Soon, the Jewish community sold their hotels and restaurants and went deeper in the Catskills. Lots of them moved to Greene and Delaware County."

"Like Amazon Indians. When populations shift closer, they hide deeper into the Amazon."

"Not as dramatically. But, yeah, that kind of happened. People are accustomed to a certain way of life."

"When did the Catskills begin to decline?"

"It started after the Second World War. Once the airlines got wise and big, the fares went down, and people stopped driving to the Catskills and instead flew to other cities or overseas. And post-Depression era generations didn't care much about saving money. They liked to enjoy their lives as much as possible. They flocked to the airports. In the 1970s and '80s, small hotels went out of business first, and by the end of the '80s the decline was evident. The glorious days of the Catskills were gone. Only mountain rats like me stayed."

It was a long day. We shared long stories about the mountain. We were a bit drunk. He's a mountain man, but I had to drive back home. We said goodbye. We knew we would see each other again soon; call it a mountain man's instinct.

At home, my wife was infuriated when I suggested buying the place. She was angry, and yelled at me. "We don't need another house. We live in a wonderful community. We have everything—a gym and a swimming pool. Our daughters live here."

Everything she said was right. I liked this house, too. But my heart was back in the mountains. I might not be a mountain rat, but I do enjoy mountain life.

"It doesn't make sense," she said. "It's a stupid idea. We cannot afford it. And it costs lots of money to renovate a dying house. It doesn't pay. I don't have time to go there. I have to babysit Max and Abby, as you know."

I tried to get her permission.

"I am retired. I like to write in a quiet environment. If you don't want to live there, I will live there alone. I won't bother you."

We argued for three weeks. Finally, she agreed to bid on the house under the condition of not spending more than a hundred thousand dollars. That was fine with me. That was my intention anyway. I've never wanted a modern, luxurious house in the mountains. I wanted to spend as little as possible. I wanted to live with the birds, deer, and fish. I believed living close to the Earth could provide inspiration for my writing. I wanted to spend the rest of my life in touch with the natural world, alone and away from the bustling city and suburbs. I didn't have many friends anyway. I wanted to be on my own. I was sure I could enjoy my time there.

I visited Ulster County the next day to bid on the house. The county tax officer was surprised to see me. The clerk said I had to pay seven years in back taxes, a total of 28,000 dollars, to buy the abandoned place. I also had to pay first year property tax, four thousand dollars plus filing fees. And he cautioned me. "It might cost you a lot more to have the electricity and water back. The storm destroyed power lines and water pipes in that area." The clerk looked at me like I was crazy. I'm sure he thought that I was either stupid or terribly impractical. But I knew what I was doing. It was within my means. I took all the papers and went home. I revisited the county office the following week and gave them a certified check. They gave me only the deed to the place—nothing more. No keys. The house had no keys. It was empty and open. "Welcome to Ulster County," the clerk said, "and good luck." He raised his eyebrows in disbelief.

I called Harry Reed and told him the news. He was surprised. He recommended that I hire a structural engineer to inspect the foundation of the house. We arranged an appointment for five days later. I returned with two padlocks and my wife. She knew how to repair a house. We had renovated our house before. I didn't do a thing. She did it all.

The engineer's name was Kevin Edwards, and he was from Sullivan County. He said he was a carpenter before he became a general contractor. He drove a pickup truck. The driveway to the house was narrow, but just wide enough for our car. I was enormously relieved about that. If the car couldn't pass, it would have been a big problem. Kevin had a wealth of knowledge about house repair. He spent nearly two hours assessing the place. He said he would give me a report and budget. I informed him that I was not ready to spend lots of money for the renovation; I was only interested in making it livable. Before we left the house, I asked Harry to hire a day worker to cut overgrown grass and mend the fence. Harry said he knew a Hispanic who did a good job for him. We were to meet again in two weeks.

I went to Home Depot to get at least some idea of what was needed for the repair work. There were lots of building materials and tools. I looked at roof materials first. I saw roof cleaners, shingles, roofing felts, and foundations for roof coating. I also saw materials for wall repair. There were various kinds of drywall and insulation fibers. There were many different kinds of mixed hardwood for flooring. Lumber was needed to reinforce the house. I didn't buy anything, because I didn't know what the engineer would say. I purchased a flashlight, a thatch rake, gloves, and basic tools. I saw a charcoal grill and a kerosene heater, but didn't buy those either.

The engineer's report was extensive, and very costly. It said the structure was not sound; it needed to be reinforced with two beams downstairs and an additional one upstairs. I had to agree for safety. The roof had to be replaced and waterproofed, and all the windows needed to be replaced. About half of the floors were rotten. Walls were not safe, partitions had to be knocked down and rebuilt. The bathrooms were not working, the kitchen cabinets were rotten and the stairs were creaking. He estimated the total cost to be 200,000 dollars. It was not unexpected, but way over my budget. I asked him if I could spend only 100,000 dollars. He said it was impossible to restore the place to a good condition for that amount. I said I didn't need a modern house. I just needed a place in bare living condition. I asked him to give me another estimate, just to repair the roof, windows, floor, walls and deck. I said the rest would be taken care of gradually as I lived there.

Kevin was not happy with my suggestion, but he said he would. He knew what I was thinking, he just didn't agree. He revised his estimate and it was

110,000 dollars. We compromised at a 105,000, and signed a contract. He said he needed two months to complete the work. It was fine with me. I could move in late April. It was a perfect time. I offered to help him, even though I was inexperienced. He said that would be appreciated. Carpenters always need extra hands, he said.

The Catskills were sleeping. The mountain was in a tight slumber under a blanket of snow. There was a stillness in the air. Mountain animals were hibernating. Birds had migrated. A few still sang, but softly. The mountain lived through a harsh three months of winter. It was well rested, and the snow had softened. The air felt like early spring, but winter was not ready to retreat. The clear, hard cold had come again. Trees trembled. The abandoned house looked beautiful during the winter months. White snow covered its ugly face. The roof might be leaking under the snow, but it was glistening. Snow drifted through the broken windows and dampened the place, but nobody could see. By mid-March, the earth felt its first break of spring. It started raining.

It turned the snow to slush, and the whole mountain became a swamp. There were clouds over the lakes and valleys. Spring had finally arrived.

Renovation started the second week of March. Kevin and his assistant unloaded lumber, shingles, plywood, and tools from the pickup truck. When they approached, the animals ran away. They knocked out a bird's nest. No mercy. It was not the animals' house anymore. It was now a human's house, my place. When people moved in, the animals had to go. They had to find another refuge. We cannot live together peacefully now. The ownership has changed. I felt sorry for them. It had been their house for the last seven years. Now they had to give up their love nest.

I was thinking about my old home close to the railroad in my childhood. One day my mother said in a sad voice, "We are going to lose our home. The authorities will seize houses here and demolish them to open a new road." We didn't have a certificate of occupancy. The government exercised eminent domain and kicked us out. The animals were also kicked out because they lived there without permission. "What permission?" they would say. "We can live wherever we want!" Poor animals, that is not the case. Man is always first, and you animals come afterwards.

I visited my house every week. Not necessarily to oversee the work, but to lend a hand if help was needed. I also needed to clean up the place. I scraped rusted railings, windowpanes, and fireplaces and painted them. I knew I was not a good painter. My wife always scolded me about that. But it was okay. It didn't have to be perfect.

Harry came one day, saw what was going on, and he seemed satisfied. He told me there might be a well somewhere on the property. The house was built before electricity and public water were supplied. This made me exceedingly happy. We looked all over and found a filled well. I worried about the water supply. The county official told me it would cost me lots of money to connect a water pipe again. A well is an old-fashioned way of life, but it was good to have one if water could not be restored. I marked the spot with white paint.

Another concern was electricity. Without power, people can hardly live. It's about more than just light. All equipment is hooked up to power: the refrigerator, washing machine, TV, computer, cell phone chargers, tools—almost everything. Since the tropical storm knocked out power lines, there's been no juice in this house. The closest house is ten minutes away. If the power company asked for tens of thousands of dollars, I wouldn't be able to afford it. I had to envision other ways to get power. I could set up a generator, but that was expensive and could break down easily; it could only be for emergencies. I asked Home Depot if there were any refrigerators not powered by electricity. They said there were none. Harry said he would call the power company and water district to get a sense of the situation.

As renovation continued, the house changed its face. It was not abandoned anymore. It was being taken care of by good hands. It looked cleaner and smarter. The dead place was reborn. It had recovered its old look. It was becoming a livable new residence, although it lacked the basic necessities of modern life. By the end of April, everything was done as the contractor had promised. The exterior of the place looked finished, but lots of work remained to be done on the interior. I hired an inexpensive Chinese handyman from Queens, and we worked together for ten days. We cleaned the fire places, bathrooms, and kitchen, converted the workroom to a study, and added a workout room.

Harry reported what he had learned about the power company and water district. It would cost us a total of fifty thousand dollars to have both—beyond my budget. Harry kindly offered use of his power and water supply whenever needed. I decided to dig the well again, put up a water tank, and connect it to the bathroom and kitchen. I could buy drinking water from the supermarket or fetch water from Harry's. I was thinking about a life without power. I could buy an ice chest to keep milk and other foods fresh. I don't watch TV much, only golf and Yankees games, so that was no big deal. I could watch the games on my cell phone. The deep valley of the Catskills had no antenna reception, but luckily Ulster was okay. I decided to heat the place with fireplaces and stoves, and cook with a gas stove and oven. It was like camping. I could still enjoy my life without power and a water supply. Why not? It was much better than what Robinson Crusoe endured. I was excited and very happy as I prepared to move into my resurrected mountain habitat. I would be the twenty-first century Robinson Crusoe of the Catskill Mountains. Not a born mountain rat, but still a rat.

It was May. The Catskills awoke from a long winter sleep. The snow remained only on the tops of the tallest mountains. The birds were back and happy, singing in the trees. Who is it that first described bird calls as cries? They are simply calling their mates by singing. The streams were whispering again, telling winter stories. The lakes and ponds were sparkling with brilliant sunshine. The sounds and smells of the mountain permeated the rejuvenated house like song and fragrance. They opened every sense, every cell in my body. I felt alive.

The house brought me back to my childhood days in Korea's deep valleys. The construction was complete. The wait was over. I never minded waiting. I needed this change at this late stage in my life. I wanted to be as close to nature as possible. For others, it might be an ugly place, but it was my dream house.

My wife hated this residence. Involuntary torture,

she declared. Why live without power and water? We deserve more than that, she said. She comes here once in a while, but doesn't stay long. It's become my house. I had to take care of everything. I read gardening magazines and did internet research. I cultivated a small garden and planted cucumbers, hot peppers, and squash. No flowers. The whole mountain is a flowerbed. Why would I need more? My wife would come on the weekends and laugh at my garden before fixing it up. I couldn't expect a good crop in the first year, but I was happy to have at least some.

I bought inexpensive wooden beds, chairs, and prepared for an open house. I invited Harry and my family. My wife brought Korean food and heated it up on the grill. Harry liked it. The kids were happy. My grandkids, Max and Abby, ran to the pond and climbed the hill. My daughters had a good time. But I sensed that they pitied me. My wife went back to our Long Island home. She couldn't miss swimming or her Korean dramas. For her, no TV and no water meant no life. Isolated from my family, I had to manage everything myself. I became a mountain rat. I decided to read and write more in this remote valley.

When my family left, the animals approached. Birds knocked on the door in the middle of the night, deer came and spoiled my vegetable garden, and rabbits hopped around. I welcomed them, but I didn't open my door. We could live together, but not in the same house. It was my place now, not theirs. I allowed the birds to build their nests in the yard or on the roof, but not inside the house. And I hated the ants.

After cutting down the tall trees, the sun lit and warmed the house most of the day. I worked there from sunrise to sunset. I went to bed early and got up at dawn. My daily life followed the sun's cycle.

One summer weekend, I invited some of my literary friends to visit. They brought barbecue beef and we grilled it in the yard. It was delicious. I had an ice box, but I kept milk and watermelon in the well. I retrieved it by hand with a pulley. I served watermelon for dessert. Everyone agreed that watermelon tasted fresher from the well, rather than when it's kept in a fridge. When darkness fell, I lit the lamps. It was not bright, but romantic. We talked about the Catskills culture and literature. My guests were fascinated. They really had a good time and wanted to come back.

Winter was another adventure. Two years ago, a big snow storm swept in from the Ohio Valley. The forecast called for six to eight inches in the New York metropolitan area and ten inches in the Catskills. I woke up in the morning, and it was already snowing. I stayed in bed with the fire roaring in the stove and watched the snow. I went to the window, looked out, but couldn't see across the road. I went outside and checked everything. All was okay. Then I saw a car approaching. I first thought my wife was coming. Then I realized it could not be her. Our grandson had been sick, and his mother had to work, so my wife was not able to make the trip. The car came near, but still I could not tell whose car it was. I stood in the snow and waited for the car. When it arrived, a literary friend from New Jersey and her husband got out.

"What made you come in this weather?" I asked, surprised. "You won't be able to leave here for a couple of days. The narrow roads here will be impassable."

"We know. When a severe snowstorm was forecasted, we worried so much about you. We ventured to come here. We thought you might starve." They unloaded lots of food from the back trunk and a warm blanket. The snow continued. Snow drifts threatened to bury my house. It snowed all night. My friends had no choice but to stay overnight. We cooked on the grill, ate well, and drank wine. The couple brought a guitar and we sang. The temperature had long since dropped below the freezing mark, and the wind blew. We didn't care about the weather outside. Inside, the house was cozy, and we had a memorable time. The animals weren't even around to bother us. They were hiding under the deep snow.

I have lived here for five years now. My wife here occasionally, bringing food and checking to see if I am okay. I am used to the mountain life. I was supposed to stay here only from spring to autumn, but now remain for most of the winter months, too. Sometimes I go home for family birthday dinners and holiday parties.

My friend and closest neighbor Harry passed away a few months ago. We shared some happy moments in these mountains. He gave me everything I needed: furniture, tools, and food. We roasted beef on the fireplace and drank wine. He was like my uncle. He knew his days were numbered. He told me I could take anything from his house. I said I only needed the electricity, which could not be moved. He died on a cold night. We had a small funeral. His son sold the house at much lower than market value.

Sometimes birds knock on my door at night. Deer roam and ask when they can enter here freely. They still believe it's their house. They love my place. Hello, animals. Don't worry too much. Be patient. I will give you back this place after I leave this beautiful world. That's why I spent so little money on the renovation; I wanted to keep this place as primitive as possible. No electricity and no water. I am sure the animals don't mind. I spend a good deal of my time here writing essays and short stories in English. I dream of creating a good piece of work. It may sound hopeless, but in my heart, it's my mission. Someone would say it's an impossible one, but I have to believe it's possible. It's sad to deny it. Animals don't understand me. They just love nature and this house. Animals own these mountains. They've lived here for thousands of years, from generation to generation. They are the mountain rats, not me.

Robbed of My Sun

It was a very hot day in Jamaica, ninety-three degrees and very humid. The sun bit the skin like it had teeth. Scantily dressed beachgoers, some nearly naked, found the heat to be quite unbearable and punishing. People swam in the water, or found shade under a tree or beneath parasols. Some sought shelter indoors to avoid the stifling heat wave.

Sharon O'Malley sat in the sun after a one-hour swim. She seemed not to care about the glaring sun. She spent the whole day at the beach, drinking soda and eating snacks. She was determined to get as much sun as possible. Sharon was a strikingly attractive woman in her late thirties, perhaps past the peak of her beauty, but not far. She had an easy smile and was well mannered. Looking at her up close, a sharp-minded person would discover her intelligence and charm. Her gaze was powerful, confident, and unwavering. She was looking toward the horizon, where the ocean and mountain meet. An innocent cloud formed a tunnel and a few ships sailed under it. She took pictures with her big Canon.

Sharon flew to Montego Bay two days earlier from New York City. It was snowing and cold in New York, twenty three degrees with five to six inches of snow. It had already snowed three times, and it was only December. Once the snow started to melt, another few inches fell to cover the ground. Sharon was sick of it, so she decided to use her timeshare vacation program. She was seduced to buy one several years earlier by a different resort in Jamaica. She regretted it at first, but then used it regularly. It was an escape from the cold and the hustle and bustle of stressful city life. She felt exceedingly happy on this Caribbean island. Jamaica always embraced the snow birds seeking a winter haven near the equator.

As soon as her plane landed, she took off her heavy jacket and changed to shorts and a light top. She felt as if she could fly like a bird.

A slim, athletic woman a bit older than Sharon sunbathed nearby. Sharon noticed that she swam for at least two hours. Sharon wondered how such a slender body stored so much energy. She swam effortlessly and gracefully. It was fun to watch. She finished her round of afternoon swimming and approached Sharon.

"Hi, I am Alice from Minnesota. Where are you from?" she asked.

"I am Sharon from New York. I live in the city that never sleeps. Always awake."

"Was it cold? Did you get snow?"

"Oh, yeah, about five inches. The temperature was not too bad. Above freezing."

"That's nothing. We had ten inches and the temperature was hovering in the low teens."

"I can imagine. I have a friend from St. Paul. She always complained about the cold. She said she would never go back there. Her body simply refused to be exposed to that cold."

"I was born there and never had a chance to get out. I've been stuck there for forty-seven years. But the summer is beautiful. It's warm and not as humid as here or in New York. Spring and autumn are gorgeous, but short."

Alice changed her expression and said, "I saw that you are not leaving the beach. You just ate and drank here. Let's go to the poolside or the indoor restaurant to have some dinner. It's miserably hot by the shore, and the bugs are coming out."

"I'd like to stay here as long as possible. Inside is cool, but I really don't want to miss the sun. I am a sun-starved woman." she said.

"Okay, I will come back with a drink and something to eat here."

"I will go with you. I don't eat much. No extra food. It hurts my health."

"That's smart thinking. That's why neither of us are heavy." They laughed.

The sun was setting. It had done its work today. Time to rest. The sky produced a spectacular display as the sun slowly sank into the water, its home sweet home. The moon reported to duty in its place high in the sky. People left the beach, one by one. Music soon filled the air on the enchanting tropical island. The two women watched the darkening ocean. It was so pristine and full of warmth. The whisper of the breeze soothed their bodies and souls.

"It's so romantic. I wish I had somebody with me," said Alice.

"Aren't you married?"

"Technically, yes. But it's virtually over. We've been separated three years. We are in the final stage of divorce."

"I am sorry to hear that. How long have you been married? Do you have kids?"

"For twenty-three long years. I have a girl and a boy. I've been robbed of my son. He took my lovely son away from me. I took my daughter. They are in college."

"Does your husband support them?"

"Husband? I don't consider him my husband anymore. He has another woman. Much younger than me. She was his secretary. He pays for their tuition. I have a decent job. I am an investment bank manager. I make as much money as he does.

Financially, I have no problems. How about you? You look like you're single."

"I am. I thought about getting married, but gave up. I don't want to be tied down. My job requires lots of traveling. I am a professional photographer. I take artistic and commercial pictures. My income fluctuates. When I have a project my earnings are good, otherwise I have to tighten my belt."

"Really? I saw your big camera."

"Do you live in a house in Minnesota?"

"Yeah, too big a house for a single woman. It's on a hill. Very good view, close to a lake. I have an abundance of sun. Unfortunately, it's the cold sun. It's fantastic in the summer, but very cold in the long winter months, from October to April."

"You are lucky. Don't complain. I have no sun. I am living in a cave. I was forced to sell my sun. You said you were robbed of your son. I was robbed of my sun."

"Living in a cave? You sold your sunlight?"

"Sounds crazy, but that's what happened. I sold my sunlight, or sun right."

"Why did you have to sell it? And who bought it?"

"The goddamn Trump Tower. We lost the battle. We filed a class action suit, but could not win. Actually, the case was settled at the last moment. They paid us one million dollars for blocking our sun. We won the battle, but lost the war."

"That's awful. So your apartment is dark, no sunlight during the daytime. Unimaginable. I am so sorry to hear that. I've never heard of this before. Where is your place in the city?"

"On the west side of Manhattan. 57th Street, a nice area. We had a beautiful view of the Hudson. We enjoyed an unparalleled river view and opulent light from the sunsets over New Jersey. We watched birds flying over the water and enjoyed five or six hours of sunshine a day. Now it's so dark and depressing. I feel like I'm living in a cave. No fresh air. We lost our light in the shadow of the towers. It's like being plunked down and surrounded by the walls of a castle. I've lived there since my college days. At first, the construction noise drove me crazy, and then I lost my sunlight. That really has been one of the cruelest blows. My bedroom and living room are now perpetually dark. I had to buy new lamps and my plants all died. It's so sad. It's not home anymore. It's a prison cell."

"I am so sorry. Let's have a drink and cheer up. We can't waste away our vacation time in a bad mood."

They walked to a poolside bar. People could drink as much as they wanted. No one was charge. Everything was all-inclusive. Some men were already drunk. They kept drinking. They just couldn't give up their love of binge drinking. It kills them, but they didn't realize it or refused to think about it. They gave a good tip to the bartender to take care of them. The bartender didn't care. No one was driving. When people were drunk they could sleep anywhere: on the couch, in their room, or even on a beach chair. Guards with rifles were protecting the tourists from local robbers. The enclosed beach community was a paradise in the jungle. The two women ordered gin and tonics and continued talking.

"So how much did you get from Trump?"

"My share was not much. About three thousand dollars. Two hundred residents shared the prize. And the attorneys took a good portion of the amount. I would give it back to Trump for my right to sunlight."

"You can't beat the giant construction companies and builders. Money talks. They push the zoning board and city officials. Why don't you move out?"

"My apartment is rent stabilized. I pay two thousand dollars a month for a big one-bedroom. I can't get the same space with that money on the Upper West Side of Manhattan."

"I have a different kind of problem in my neighborhood. There is an old Catholic church close to my home. As you know, the church is dying these days. People say 'Oh my God' a hundred times a day, but they don't go to church. No congregation. The church is empty even on Sunday. For years, the church bells tolled twice a day—at noon and again at 6 p.m. But when a new pastor arrived he stepped up the chime schedule to thirteen times a day. More on the weekends. Neighbors complained to the church, but they didn't listen. The worst came after a few days later, after the dispute was reported by a local newspaper—the church bells rang all night. I woke up from a dead sleep. It was in retaliation. I couldn't believe it."

"Like Big Ben. It's more than the calling of the mosque. They do that five times a day. For whom do the bells toll? For the people or for the church? If the bells tortured the church's neighbors, the church would not be a savior but rather a destroyer. Fortunately, we don't have the towers problem. If any building blocked my sun I would bomb it and go to jail. It's ridiculous. The sun belongs to everybody. It's not just for the rich. So we all have bad neighbors. We are powerless people in a roaming jungle."

At that moment the bartender jumped in. He overheard the conversation. He couldn't believe what he had heard.

"I heard you sold your sun. We have too much sun here in Montego Bay. Always pure and hot. It's free. You can enjoy the sun here or bring the sunshine to New York. We also have lots of churches in Jamaica. The church bells toll twice a day. They don't have to toll anymore. Folks always go to church on Sundays. What a different world you live in. It's beyond my comprehension. I hate this sun. Too hot and it makes my skin dark. I wish my skin was as white as yours. This goddamn sun burns my body.

"I am a trapped tropical bird. I cannot fly to America. They won't issue a visa for me. I envy snow birds like you. You can fly to whatever weather you like," the bartender said.

"Don't complain. You should appreciate it. It's your privilege. It's a gift from God. We had the same privileges. But somebody took them away from us. They robbed us. It's unfair. It happened under the name of development. The sun was given by God. God doesn't say anything. Maybe God doesn't know."

"There is only the sun. It's for everybody. I like my summer sun in Minnesota. It's so friendly and caring. But I don't love the winter sun. It's too far away, and too cold. I wish I had a warm sun during the winter. The sun doesn't move. The Earth moves. We are living on a different corner of the planet. The sun is always there. People are not. We have to follow the sun. Like sunflowers."

Sharon stayed another week in Montego Bay. She stored the sun in her body, in her face, on her arms, legs and stomach. She put the hot sun in her pockets, too. Alice, the Minnesotan woman, spent as much time as she could under the blazing sun with her new friend. They wanted to bring the Jamaican sun back to where they lived. They couldn't. They burned their bodies instead. They brought home the gift of nature from a tropical island. They were refreshed and happy, but only until they became exposed to the cold in their homes. Sharon was robbed of her sun. But she recovered it. Only temporarily.

Death of a Deacon

Deacon John Yoo was a good man, a devoted and responsible husband and father—the pillar of his family. His life had been as orderly and spotless as his home. But an unexpected visit by his church pastor changed everything. It happened on Tuesday, February 23, 2010, in Atlanta, Georgia.

Deacon Yoo, his wife Esther, and his two daughters, Ashley and Emily, had just finished their dinner. There was a knock at the front door. When the deacon opened the door, Pastor Kim stood there.

"Oh my goodness! Pastor Kim! What a surprise!"

"You're home. Sorry I didn't let you know in

advance. I have something to discuss with you."

The pastor apologized to the deacon's family for the unannounced visit. He sat on the couch and prayed for the family. Then he asked to speak privately with Deacon Yoo. They went upstairs to Deacon Yoo's home office.

"Deacon Yoo, I need your help. I want you to be involved in the construction of the education center. It's God's work."

"What do you mean? I believe Elder Park is doing a good job."

"He is good, but not reliable. He is not living up to our expectations. I think he needs your help. As you know, an education center is necessary for the growth of our church. Right now, we are short on space for classrooms and parents are hesitant to send their children to our church."

"Pastor, I know that. That's why we have a construction committee and Elder Park is the chair. He is very capable. He knows the community, speaks good English, and he is very competent. Nobody in our church is as qualified as he."

"That's true. But there is no progress. He loves

to talk, but he is not a man of action. He lacks enthusiasm for the project."

"Well, it takes time. We formed the committee only six months ago. We aren't even halfway done. We are moving in that direction. He needs more time."

"We cannot wait too long. Our church is not growing. In the last three months, we haven't added any new members. Without a good education annex, our church cannot grow. Young families flock to the bigger churches, which have better education systems. An education center is the driving force for the expansion of our church."

"Pastor, it's a big responsibility. I am not suitable for this daunting task. I am not rich, I don't speak English well, and I don't have much time. It's more than a full-time job. Elder Park is semi-retired, sociable, and, most importantly, he is well-known in the community."

"We don't need a celebrity. We need someone who can deliver the promise. I have thought about this for the last two months. I strongly believe you are the right person. We need new blood. That's you. The Lord is calling you. You should answer His call. Of course, it's a difficult task. When it's done, you will be very happy. You will be remembered forever in this church. Please take on this responsibility."

"Pastor, I am not an elder. The chair should be an elder. That doesn't mean I want to be an elder. No way. I will remain a deacon forever. Actually, I don't even deserve to be a deacon."

"Then how about this? Elder Park stays on as chair and you take the co-chair role. But you will be doing the important work. He will only hold the title."

"I have to talk to my wife. My daughter is going to college this year. Another one goes to college the year after. I have to work hard to save money."

"Deacon, it is the Lord's word. You cannot disobey Him. Our church has to grow. Not for us. This is for the expansion of God's world. Please accept it."

The deacon didn't say a word. He was dead silent, motionless, and stared at the ceiling. Pastor Kim was deep in thought, his face like a stone. He didn't stir. The two men spent more than ten minutes without saying a word. The pastor broke the silence. "Deacon, please help me. Not only for our church, but for God."

Deacon Yoo said in a feeble voice, "I will do it. If it's

God's work."

When the pastor left the house it was 10 p.m. and raining. Darkness surrounded his slender body. But he seemed relieved and happy. He sang gospel songs as he drove home.

Deacon Yoo stayed in his office after the pastor left. A thousand questions crossed his mind. Why was he here? Why me? Why did I say yes? Why didn't I talk to my wife first? Can I do the job? How can I support my family? Can I save enough to send my daughters to college? He regretted his reckless decision without his wife's consent. But it was too late. It was like spilled milk. He couldn't reverse his decision. At that moment, his wife entered the room.

"Why did Pastor Kim come at this odd hour?"

He didn't answer immediately. He looked up the ceiling with a heavy sigh.

"He was talking about the education center. He said our church needed my dedication."

"What does he mean? We already have a committee and Elder Park is heading it."

"He thinks Elder Park is not doing his job."

"Did he want you to do the work? It is a big-time job and a controversial one. It consumes lots of hours."

"I know. That's why I hesitated. But he pleaded to me to take the responsibility."

"Did you accept it?"

"Yes. Sorry I didn't get your permission. I wanted to talk to you first, but …"

"But what? You can't do that without consulting me. I am your wife. It's not a matter of something small. It's a serious job. We built a new church two years ago. Our church is in huge debt. The congregation members are complaining about the church's finances. How could you accept it without asking me?"

"I am sorry. It was my mistake. But it was not God's mistake. God never makes mistakes. As the pastor said, God called me for this work."

His wife looked at him with a skeptical face. "Are you okay? Did you think about your family? Do you believe the church will feed us if we were starving? Did you think about our daughters' college education? Call the pastor and say you changed your mind."

"I can't. The decision has been made. I can't lie to God. Don't worry too much. The Lord will protect us. He will take care of us."

"Who is more important to you, the church or your family? You should be practical. You're a husband and father first. Church is next. Not the other way."

"The pastor's word is like God's word. He conveyed God's words to me. I already promised the Lord. I can't take it back. I will try my best to do God's work and to support my family."

She looked at him with a wounded expression. She closed the door and went downstairs. She sobbed.

January and February passed and spring arrived without delay. The winter had been full of cold rain and wild winds. Atlanta was clouded in a pervasive gloom and depression. The real estate boom was long gone. The Georgia government enforced tough immigration policies and most Hispanic people left town. Many small retail stores, including Korean businesses, lost customers. There were numerous empty stores in the downtown area. A fresh wave of despair swept the city. Some old folks compared this with the Civil War years. Back then, the town was crowded with wounded soldiers and refugees. Supplies were inadequate for the crying needs of the stricken city. Atlanta was not friendly to newcomers in those days. But now, spring had arrived. It brought bright sunshine to the neglected land. People could see a silver lining in the clouds. Deacon Yoo was working on house repairs. He was a carpenter-turned-contractor. He couldn't get a big contract, only small house renovations and work fixing stores. His business was good until about five to six years ago. At that time, Georgia was a part of the real estate boom. Koreans from cold weather flocked to Atlanta. Big Korean supermarket chains opened, Korean Airlines flew every day to Seoul. People could hear Korean everywhere and they could get Korean newspapers without paying a cent. Atlanta became the third largest Korean community after Los Angeles and New York. Deacon Yoo joined the migration.

The deacon's family moved here from New Jersey about ten years ago. They liked the warm weather. They were tired of the bustle of the big city. A house here was much cheaper than one in New Jersey. They could buy a million dollar house with only 350,000 dollars in Georgia. Lots of retirees moved here from the Midwest and northeast. Real estate agents were busy. The deacon had lots of work and saved a lot of money. He and his family were happy. Then the real estate business declined, the prices of houses plummeted and the market was frozen. Young people went back to the places where they had come from, and only the professionals and retirees stayed. Deacon Yoo couldn't find work. Fortunately, Esther had a decent job. She was a registered nurse. She worked in the hospital from eight to four. When her husband's business was no good, she had a second job for supplemental income. She worked in a nursing home two days a week. They were hard working people.

Growing up in Korea, John Yoo was from a Christian home. His mother was a good Christian. He worked as a manager for a ladies apparel manufacturing company in Korea. He was in his thirties then. There were endless labor disputes at that time. The gap between the rich and the poor was widening. The owners tried to expand their enterprises and workers demanded a bigger share of the pie.

The company had about two hundred employees, and most of them were females in their teens or twenties. They worked more than ten hours a day. Their wages were raised but still fell short of their expectations. They took part in the various strikes organized by the labor unions. There was no peace in the workplace. Tensions were high, animosity between the management and the union ran deep. Some good-hearted people tried to build a bridge for reconciliation, but failed.

One day the volcano erupted: the workers called for a strike, occupied the factory, and broke some machinery. The management called in the police. They stood in opposition for three days. Finally, the authorities decided to drag away the striking workers from the factory. Two young female workers jumped off the building and died. Workers blamed John, for he was on the management side and didn't try to heed their complaints. He was shocked and heartbroken. He couldn't bear the death of the young, innocent girls. He quit and decided to immigrate to the United States with his family.

It was after this move that John began to embraced God. He went to a nearby church, read the Bible, and didn't miss service. He became a devoted Christian. His faith healed his wounds from the suicides of those two women. That was fifteen years ago. Ashley was three years old and Emily was one year old then. Esther got a nursing job in New Jersey and John took work as a carpenter. He had been a good, honest, and responsible carpenter. He earned a good reputation. Then he became a contractor. He hired a few Hispanic people and received small house repair jobs. His business was good. He was looking for a house for his family. It was beyond their means. Then the Georgia wind blew. One of his close friends moved to Atlanta. He joined the migration wave again.

Elder Chung called Deacon Yoo. "Congratulations! I heard you got a big job. You will be chair of the construction committee, which is the most important position in our church. The pastor just called me. We will have a meeting this Saturday to approve it.

I guess Pastor Kim likes you a lot. Everybody in our church will look up to you. You are a big shot now."

Deacon Yoo couldn't believe what he had just heard.

"Who said I will be the chair? My job is helping Elder Park. No more than that. And what do you mean I am the pastor's favorite? I don't want to be perceived as his right-hand man by the church members."

"You know. Rumors never stop spreading among church people. People are saying Elder Park is out and you are in charge now. Pastor Kim never liked him from the start. He thought Park was not responsible. Now, you are the man."

"I don't need the church members' attention. That's a burden. I just want to help a little bit."

"You should watch out. Lots of congregations are not happy about the direction our church is heading. We have almost a million dollars of debt. I have no idea where the money will come from. But he doesn't listen. All he thinks about is the education center. He firmly believes having an education annex is the only way our church can grow."

"Please disregard the unfounded rumor. I am a small guy. I don't want to be engulfed in church politics. I have no ambition of being a big shot in our church. I accepted the responsibility because the pastor said it was God's order. I couldn't be against the Lord."

"Anyway, we will appoint you the chair or co-chair of the committee. But it will not be easy. Lots of elders will present their differing opinions."

Deacon Yoo couldn't continue his work. He found he was in the center of a storm. In the past, he had avoided being involved in controversial situations, but now he was entrapped. He prayed, "Lord, I am a poor, weak man. Please give me the courage and power to carry out my mission."

The church had an elders' meeting. It was the highest organization in the church and consisted of six acting elders and two anointed deacons. Deacon Yoo was not a member of this body. Pastor Kim had already persuaded the elders, so the appointment was not expected to face much resistance. Pastor Kim stressed the importance of the construction of the education building and proposed to select Deacon Yoo as a co-chair of the committee. He said, "The chair's responsibility is too heavy, too much for one individual. It needs to be divided into two parts. Elder Park will assume the external affairs dealing with the fire department, county office, and other local authorities. And Deacon Yoo will take on the financing and construction part."

Elder Park raised no objections. He was released from a heavy burden he had carried for several months. He was still the chair and could represent the church. All the headaches were on Deacon Yoo now.

Deacon Yoo was introduced to the elders. He made a short speech: "I may not be the right person for this enormous task. I will try to fulfill God's work. May God bless this holy church." He felt it was his fate—pre-destined. The elders gave him warm applause and shook his hand. He looked solemn and as resolute as stone. Pastor Kim was extremely satisfied.

When the meeting was over Elder Park said to Deacon Yoo in the church parking lot, "Congratulations, Deacon Yoo. Don't kill yourself. It's a massive job. I will tell you what's going to happen. The pastor will push you relentlessly. When we have the education center and our church grows, he will be about retirement age. He wants to remain as an honorary senior pastor for many years. He might think this church is God's place, but also it's his place. They are hardly separable." Then he left. He didn't look sad. He seemed he knew the pastor a lot more than Deacon Yoo. Elder Park penetrated the pastor's mind.

Two weeks passed. The pastor called Deacon Yoo almost every day. They mapped out the strategy for the fundraising drive with two other elders who were the pastor's confidants. The budget was two million dollars, which was a huge amount for the church and a financially stricken community. The church had already raised three million dollars over the last few years for the construction of the main church building. Pastor Kim was unwavering. He showed no signs of retreating. "This is the Lord's order. We have to accomplish this. Not a single one of God's great works ever came easily. We will face severe opposition. There are many hurdles to jump. We have to be stubborn. We have to persuade the church members and lead them. God is on our side. I will be in the front. Please follow me." Deacon Yoo was frightened.

"I have no choice. The die is cast," the deacon murmured.

The fundraising campaign started. The pastor asked the congregation members to pledge their portion of contribution, which was common practice. He pushed very hard, not giving any signs of relenting. His sermons focused on the education center for seven straight weeks. No break. Every Sunday he was talking about money, money, money. He said, "The Lord wants this. It's God's will. We are doing this for the next generation. If you love your children, you should join this holy campaign."

The first week was not so hard. He gave the Old John Brown story to the church members. Old John Brown was an abolitionist. He believed slavery was against God's word. He was a man of the Bible. He knew every section of the Old and New Testaments. He firmly believed owning slaves was a sin. He had twenty-two children from two wives. His sons and daughters followed his crusade to free slaves. He organized militia to attack slave holders. He killed a lot of people for his cause. Old John Brown's army attacked the U.S. military armory in Virginia to seize guns and ammunition and mobilize African American people to fight against slavery. His army was defeated by the federal troops and he was hung. But he was proud of himself, because he answered God's call to fight evil. The old man was a lunatic, but he was a good, kind lunatic. He was a true soldier for God. He was crazy, but pure to the truth.

The pastor said at the end of his sermon, "Old John Brown gave his life for God's order. Not only his life, but also his children's lives. After his death, the Civil War began. He planted the seeds of liberation for the African American people in this country. Congregation, our church needs you. Not your blood, but your contributions for the education building. It may not be easy. But your donations and sacrifice will be remembered forever. It's God's order. Please listen to His voice and join the sacred task."

The pastor delivered stunning news in his second Sunday sermon. He said, "A deacon donated thirty thousand dollars in cash for the construction of the education center. He is not a rich man. He is not a doctor or a lawyer. He gave a big portion of his family's savings for future generations. What would you do for God's work? Will you join his contribution or ignore it? Your donation goes to God's world. You cannot carry any money with you when you die. Everybody comes to this world with empty hands and leaves with empty hands. If you donate your money, it would be used for God's work. Please participate in our great cause."

When the church service was over, people whispered, "Who gave that much money? And it's cash. What if somebody reports it to the IRS?"

Esther Yoo was shocked upon hearing about the cash donation. She rushed to her house to check the safe and found thirty thousand dollars missing. She was astonished. They had saved the money for their daughters' college tuition. She wept and waited for her husband. He had been late every day since he took the co-chair position. She was red-hot with rage. It was unbearable to think about what would happen.

Esther was a slim and ordinary woman. She was a compassionate person. She was a good wife and caring Mom. She was humble and unassuming.

She didn't wear expensive clothing or jewelry, but sometimes she stunned her friends with a flash of raw beauty. She was a kitchen Mom. She liked to cook and was happy when her husband and kids enjoyed the food she had made. She was a sewing Mom, too. She repaired a pair of her daughter's jeans in less than twenty minutes and she did it better than anybody else. She had quick and magical hands. Her family was first and foremost to her. She was stern with her daughters, but not a "Tiger mom." She tried to give them as much freedom as possible. Her daughters were excellent students. Ashley was an honor student, in the top two percent in her class and editor of the school paper. The expectation of her school was that she would get into an Ivy League school. Emily was two years younger than Ashley. She was on the honor roll, too. Esther always told them, "Do the right thing."

Esther liked the quiet manner of her husband. She supported his decisions most of the time and rarely argued with him. There were times she disagreed with his thinking, but she didn't pick a fight. She believed every minor issue would settle itself with the passage of time. It turned out to be true.

Esther was also a wise consumer. She knew exactly which stores had the best bargains. Whenever she had free time, she scoured through the nooks and crannies of department stores for deals. Her friends always asked her about shopping bargains and deals.

Pastor Kim's unexpected visit to her house created a dramatic turn for the family. John was not the same husband. He seemed haunted. He didn't talk, lost his smile, and he was deadly serious. Esther was sad and felt like she lost her husband. She was mad at the church. She believed she was robbed of her husband. Whenever she saw his unsmiling, stern face her heart was broken. Her daughters noticed the abrupt change in their father. He was not home for most of the day. He went to the early morning service with his tired body and came home late at night. They couldn't figure out what he was thinking.

Deacon Yoo felt the heat. He saw the tears of his wife and despair of his daughters. Nobody said a word in the house. No laughter, no merry music, no talking. It was like a cloister in a deep mountain.

Deacon Yoo sensed he wasn't as good to his family as he had been before. He knew his family avoided him. But he couldn't retreat. His hands were tied, his mind overwhelmed by the invisible fetters. He realized the future of his family was up in the air. He sobbed alone in his room and always prayed, "Lord, please rescue me. I am following your orders. Please make my family embrace the Holy Spirit." Then he went to sleep in his office. He had nightmares, wandering in the distant world.

He got up in the wee hours, picked up the elderly, and went to the early morning Bible study. He didn't care if it was raining or not. It was his routine. He believed it was God's call. Pastor Kim seldom led the morning service. That was the job of the assistant pastors and missionary women.

Deacon Yoo came home at about 10 p.m. He went upstairs quietly. Esther heard his footsteps and knocked on his door. He looked exhausted and pale. He seemed to have lost at least five pounds in the last few months. She felt pity for him, but she couldn't hold her anger.

"You took out thirty thousand dollars and gave it to

the pastor. How could you do that? Is it your money or our money?"

"I didn't give that money to him. I gave it to God. It's not my money. It's not your money either. It's God's money. It's less than two percent of what we need. Of course it's important for our family. I was in anguish. God appeared in my dreams and ordered my contribution. I believe our church members will follow my example. As a chair of the committee I had to do that."

She was dumbfounded. "What's the matter with you? Are you the same husband and father? Are you out of your mind?"

"I know what I am thinking and what I am doing. Please don't look at me with that strange face. I am the same man. But I've changed after the Holy Spirit touched me. Now the Lord leads me. I am just following His orders."

"What did the Lord tell you? Did the Lord order you to neglect your family and give all our money to the church? How come your God is so different from mine? I believe in God, too. My God never told me not to take care of my family. He wants us to love and care for our family. I think the pastor is leading you astray. He has filled your heart with delusions. Please wake up. Go back to the caring husband and father I once knew." She wept.

"Honey, please stop. You can't accuse the church and God. God is behind us, and will protect our family. I answered His call. The Lord will take care of us. The Lord is great. Jesus owns our church. It's His house. I am trying to improve God's house. That's a mission given by God. I understand you are frustrated now. I am sure you will understand me later on. You will be respected by the church members."

"I don't care about that. I won't go to church anymore. I don't want to face the pastor. What you believe in is not the real God. It is a deception."

"Please stop. That's blasphemy. You will be punished severely. Oh, Lord, please forgive her."

Deacon Yoo cried. He thought his wife was not right. Esther cried too. She felt her husband was not right. They cried for different reasons. They had different faiths. There's only one God. They accepted God differently according to their own perspectives.

Esther didn't go to church the next few weeks. Her church friends divulged to her what was going on. Everybody knew Deacon Yoo gave the cash to the pastor. He hoped the congregation would follow the deacon's initiative. Pastor Kim reported every Sunday the pledged amounts of the church members. People were sick of it. Some complained, "Are we debtors? Why does he push us so hard?" Some people stopped coming to church. The women members expressed pity to Esther. They knew what a good woman she was. One day when Esther was about to finish her hospital shift, the pastor's wife came to visit her. She was quite different from other pastors' wives. She didn't come to church much, didn't stand with the pastor to say hello at the end of service. Some people didn't even recognize her. Esther saw her a couple of times, so she knew her.

"Mrs. Yoo, how have you been? I didn't see you the last few weeks. I know how hard everything is for you. Please come to church. Pastor Kim and the other church members are worried about you."

Esther didn't say a word. The pastor's wife didn't seem sincere. She just conveyed her husband's message to her. Esther saw the lies in her eyes.

"Whether or not I go to church doesn't make a difference. Thank you for seeing me. I will attend service when the time comes."

Esther received more calls from her church friends. They told her that women members were critical of the pastor, which hurt the church and made Deacon Yoo very nervous. Esther felt uneasy. She went to the service the following week. That was her. She supported her husband even though she didn't approve of his demeanor. The pastor was happy to see her, and so was Deacon Yoo.

Pastor Kim was a small man. He was five-foot -seven, weighed 150 pounds. He graduated from the Presbyterian Theology College in Korea and served three years as a military pastor. He seemed proud of having served in the military, mentioning it more than necessary. He had started a new church near Seoul, but it was not a success. He decided to come to the United States to seek opportunity when he was thirty-two years old. He was hired as a young missionary by a Korean church in southern

California. It was the peak of Korean immigration. Every day, new immigrants arrived. When they arrived, their friends brought them to a nearby church and introduced them to the pastor. Then church members helped them find an apartment, register their kids in public school, and get jobs, mostly at Korean small businesses. Small church pastors were like immigration guides at the time. They drove church vans carrying new settlers' huge suitcases. Sometimes they provided shelter until new arrivals could find an apartment. They were like family.

Pastor Kim taught Sunday school. He not only taught the Bible, but also English, even though his English was not great. He went to the Southern California Theology Seminary while he worked for the church. Upon graduating, he moved to another church as an assistant pastor. He served for eight years and learned how to manage an immigrant church. It was in the late 1990s that he was called by an Atlanta Korean church to serve as a pastor in the late 1990s. His dream had come true. He was forty-three years old. The Atlanta Korean community had started to grow. It picked up steam as the years passed. In early 2000, the Korean migration boom reached its peak in Georgia. It was like a new wave of immigration, reminiscent of the 1970s and 1980s in Los Angeles and New York.

When Pastor Kim started his mission for the church, it had about four hundred congregation members. It wasn't a small number, but he wasn't satisfied with it. The church had a modest building, but no building for the children. He worked really hard. His church was his new holy business. He opened the church doors early in the morning, cleaned the place, and answered every call.

Most American churches were losing members at that time, but Korean churches were thriving. They started to rent empty church space from American churches for a small cost. People said new churches emerged overnight. It was like the budding of a new bamboo tree after the rain. There were so many tiny churches in the Korean neighborhood that people compared them to tea rooms or coffee houses in 1970s Korea. There were culture clashes everywhere. American church members didn't like the smell of

Korean food, and kids were running around. Korean churches eagerly wanted to have their own worship places. Every church pushed their members to buy or build a new church. Wherever Korean immigrants lived, there were churches.

According to the Korean Christian Press survey, there were 4,300 Korean churches in this country in 2010. California had the most, about fourteen hundred. New York and New Jersey were next with seven hundred. Georgia had more than two hundred churches. The average number of registered members of a congregation was about two hundred. When people met at a restaurant or somebody's house, they loved to talk of their churches: "Which church do you go to? Who is the pastor? How many members does your church have? How much does your church collect a week? Is your church quiet? No fighting? Our church is in an ugly fight. It will probably split into two soon."

There were endless scandals in the churches. People were fighting over the church property and hegemony. There were some sex scandals between pastors and women church members, too. When people asked, "How could this happen in a church?" someone else would answer, "You know, a pastor is not God, he is human. Anything can happen in the church. God doesn't know what's going on. He has no control over it."

Pastors in big Korean churches started to retire in early 2000. They were founders of the churches, responsible for their growth and the construction of huge church buildings. They were deeply involved in the selection process of their successors. It was like their corporation. They hoped to be remembered as a pioneer of the church and wanted to exercise some influence over the new pastors. The churches had memorable farewell services and elevated the departing pastor as a senior pastor. Most of the churches supported them financially for the rest of their lives. It was like a pension plan.

Nobody could read the pastor's mind correctly, but old church officials had an acute eye for seeing the pastor's thoughts. Elder Park was one of them. He suspected Pastor Kim's real motivation for his zeal for the education center. Pastor Kim was now fifty-three years old. He would be over sixty when the church had an education building and grew to one of the biggest churches in the Atlanta Korean community. He would retire then and be known as the real legend of the church. He would expect the church to take care of him in his retirement.

Elder Park was smart enough not to be caught up in such an enormously difficult situation. He was watching what was going on after he released himself from the burden. He was happy to be an outsider. He knew the church culture well. The pastor was on top of the organization. He chose elders he could handle, controlled church finances, and hired associate pastors and missionaries. He was like a big boss of a company. Every staff member of the church had to obey to him. There was no genuine discussion in the church. It was always one-way communication. Nobody could rebut the pastor's sermons, even if they disagreed. They could complain at their homes, but not in front of their pastor. It was not a culture of respect and trust. Above all else, they had to obey God. Pastors believed they were the messengers between God and the congregation. Pastor Kim was no exception. He knew what he was doing. He knew people were complaining. But he firmly believed that when everything was over people would appreciate what he had done. He said to himself, "Every great feat was achieved through challenges and sacrifice. When we cross the desert we will see the oasis. Fortunately, I have Deacon Yoo. He is the true son of God. I need more people like Deacon Yoo in our church."

That following spring, a good thing and a bad thing happened to Deacon Yoo's family. Ashley was accepted to both Columbia and Duke Universities. Her mother was very proud of her and told the news to her colleagues in the hospital. They all congratulated her and wished her daughter good luck. But Esther's mind was heavy. Ashley wanted to go Columbia, because she liked New York City. Ashley didn't tell the good news to her Dad. It was hard to see him, his mind was so engrossed in the church construction. Esther didn't know what to do. She knew it would cost them fifty thousand dollars a year. They had little savings after he gave away the thirty thousand dollars. Ashley couldn't apply for a scholarship, because Esther reported eighty thousand dollars in earnings from her two jobs. They were poor, but not poor enough to qualify for financial aid. Ashley knew about this well. She said, "Mom, don't worry. I will go to the University of Georgia. It's not an expensive college and my school adviser said I have a good chance of getting a scholarship. Upon graduating from college, I want to go to a good law school."

"Sorry, Ashley. If your Dad supported our family as he had before, it would be no problem, but he is a different man now. The church took your Dad away from us."

"I can see that, Mom. I know you are disappointed. I hope he realizes how important his family is."

"He's getting worse. He hasn't given me any money these last few months. I heard he fixed a church member's house and when they paid him, he gave it back to them to donate to the church."

"Is that true? I can't believe it. I don't understand what he is thinking."

"Ashley, I will try to send you to Columbia. Maybe I can work more hours."

"Mom, please don't even think about it. You are

working more than you can handle. Think about your health. Nobody will suffer and die for you. Forget Dad. Take care of yourself."

At that time their phone rang. It was from the hospital. Deacon Yoo was injured and brought to the emergency room. They were stunned and asked about his condition. The nurse said the injury wasn't that serious, and he could leave the hospital the next day. Esther and Ashley rushed to the hospital.

When they arrived, the deacon was getting all kinds of tests done. His face was swollen, his right leg injured. He said he was hit by a heavy machine. The owner of the house saw the accident and quickly called an ambulance. They met the doctor. The EKG had revealed his heart was not normal and they recommended further tests. Otherwise, he was okay and would be fine in a few days. Deacon Yoo slept that night at the hospital and came home the next day. The nurse told them that he read the Bible and prayed whenever he was alone. She said she'd never seen a more religious patient.

Ashley entered her father's room the next morning.

"Dad, how do you feel? You still don't look okay. Do

you need anything?"

"I feel better. I had a good night's sleep. God is protecting me so that I can finish His work."

"What work, Dad?"

"The education center. He will save me until I finish the great project."

"Please don't kill yourself. You are more important than anything else. By the way, I got accepted to Columbia. Will you support me?"

"I wish I could, but … I can't do anything until we are done with the education building."

"Dad, what is more important? Me or the stupid education annex? I never understand what you have in your mind. I want my old Dad who played with me, brought us to Disney World, watched movies with us, and ate out with Mom, Emily, and me. You look like a ghost, not a real person."

"Ashley, don't accuse me. I have changed. I am living for God's cause."

"What kind of God do you believe in? I have faith, too. My God never told me to abandon my family. My English mission pastor always said family came first and that's God's teaching. We need you. We need your love, your support, and your money"

"Ashley, don't curse the Holy Redeemer. We are living by the Lord's word. Only He knows what we are doing. He will judge us ultimately."

"You sound like a scared man. Who made you such a miserable man? I don't care about the final judgment. I did nothing wrong in my life. I always tried to do the right thing. I helped people. Why should I be punished? What you believe in is not the real God."

"Don't complain against God. That's challenging God's authority."

"I am not denying God. I am challenging somebody who is manipulating your pure mind. I knew you took a chunk of money out of our safe. With that money, I could have gone to Columbia. Now I have to go a public college to save money. Mom is saying she could work extra hours for my tuition, but how could I let her? And you don't care about me. All you ever talk about is the education center, church, church, church. I hate it all." She cried and rushed out of his room.

Deacon Yoo prayed as soon as she left, "Lord, please

forgive your young daughter. She will repent for her sin."

Deacon Yoo recovered under the warm care of his wife. But they didn't talk much. A wide and deep river was flowing between them. There was no room for them in the same world. Ashley avoided her father and he didn't seem to care much. They were living in separate worlds: him in outer space, the others in the real world.

Deacon Yoo started to work again, but he didn't bring in any money. He did house repair work for church members, but declined to take their money and told them to donate it to the church. He was a church man and a Bible man, not a family man.

The fundraising campaign didn't go as the pastor wanted. The total amount raised didn't even reach a quarter-million dollars that year. The total pledged amount was another quarter-million, but there was no way to know when the church members would actually bring the money in. Everything was delayed and it made the pastor nervous. He pushed again in his sermon, "Our students are the lost children. They are wandering in the wilderness. We have to give them a comfortable space to make them learn God's word. Please open your kind hearts and donate your money. Storing treasure in your own house is no use in God's world."

One student said when he heard the story, "We are not wandering. We have classrooms and good teachers teaching us the Bible."

Esther noticed her husband's health was deteriorating. He was short of breath and occasionally complained of dizziness. She told him, "Forget the church and take care of yourself. Go exercise and visit a doctor to check your heart. You may need another EKG. Take an ultrasound."

Deacon Yoo didn't listen. He said, "Don't worry about me. God is protecting me. He will save me until we finish our education building." Esther didn't say a word. She studied his face, as white as paper. She was sad but couldn't do anything. He was not the same man.

Three years passed. Ashley was a junior in the

University of Georgia and her sister Emily entered the same school. The deacon had been the same church man, the pastor's favorite. He didn't care about his family. He didn't know how his wife managed the family finances and how his daughters were doing at school. All he cared about was the church. The fundraising drive stalled. They had raised about a half-million dollars but were well short of what they needed. They had to collect at least that much more to start the construction.

The Atlanta Korean community stopped growing. The real estate business was in deep recession. Housing prices kept falling every year. Unsold housing inventory was piling up, and people left town. Some retirees moved in from up north, but not good enough to boost the community. New big Korean supermarket chains opened, competition was fierce, and consumers took advantage.

Ashley enjoyed her college life. She maintained an excellent academic record and prepared for law school. She hoped to attend law school at Duke University. She met her boyfriend Justin Walker in her junior year. He was a law student at Duke. He was an articulate man from Alabama. His Dad was a law firm partner in Birmingham. Justin had heard about Ashley's family situation. It was beyond his imagination. He couldn't understand the dynamics of the Korean church. It was all strange to him. His family was Christian, too. But they didn't go to the early morning service. It was absolutely voluntary. They were never pushed to offer donations for any reason.

Justin loved Ashley dearly. He liked her charm, intelligence, tenderness, and most importantly, that she was kind-hearted. His parents loved her, too. They visited his Alabama home and their summer house in Maine.

Ashley introduced Justin to Emily and her mother, but not to her father. She didn't want to show his haggard, stricken face to him. Esther liked Justin a lot. She thought he was well-mannered, clean-faced, agreeable and smart. She particularly liked his gentlemanly attitude toward her daughter. She didn't notice his toughness as a law student then. Upon graduating from the University of Georgia, Ashley entered Duke Law School and Justin graduated from

Duke that year. He passed the bar exam in Georgia and Alabama. He started to work for a prestigious law firm in Atlanta.

Two more years passed. The church finally started construction on the education building. They got a loan from a Korean bank. The pastor and Deacon Yoo were extremely happy. The deacon rediscovered his long-forgotten smile. He stood next to the pastor and broke ground. All kinds of equipment arrived, construction noise hit the neighborhood, and dirt flew all over. Neighbors began to complain. They called the town office and reported to the local police department. The authorities came to the site to look into it, but couldn't stop the work. The church had acquired the legitimate construction permits. The church extended its hand to make peace with the neighborhood. Deacon Yoo oversaw the construction work and reported every detail to Pastor Kim. He often didn't go home and slept in the church. His family didn't care much.

Winter came. The frigid blast disrupted people's life in the South and the Northeast. The snow made roads impassable and forced some schools to prepare to keep students overnight. Many people in the metro Atlanta area slept in offices and hotels. Farther south, snow and sleet were as unwelcome as unexpected. It might have been fun for kids, but was bad for businesses and residents. It snowed only a few inches, but it caused as much damage as a foot of snow in the Northeast. Cars were abandoned on highways and people walked to their homes. Atlanta was in a state of emergency.

The pastor of the church called Deacon Yoo and other loyal church members. "We should clear the snow as soon as possible. And we should help our neighbors. They complain about our construction. Now is the time to make amends. If we clear the roads, they will be appreciative and stop complaining. Let's mobilize all our available snow removal equipment. Fortunately, we do have some snow plows. Let's do it all night."

Deacon Yoo took the lead. He called the young church members to join in the work. He didn't realize how exhausted he was. He didn't eat well; he wasn't rested. He was devastated physically and emotionally.

He collapsed that night at church. A church member called 911, but the ambulance didn't arrive fast enough to save him because of all the falling snow. He died that night. Perhaps he saw Jesus on his deathbed, but he didn't leave any words. His gave his life for the church. He didn't see the completion of the education center. The snow ceased when he died. The wind wept for his death. And the birds cried in the empty dark sky. It was deadly quiet and eerie.

The deacon's family received a call from the hospital. They rushed to the hospital. He was taken to the morgue. They met the pastor. He gave his deepest sympathy for the loss of a good husband, father, and Christian.

A local newspaper reported his death the next morning. It said Deacon Yoo died of a heart attack while clearing the snow for the neighborhood. The newspaper described him as a Good Samaritan. It didn't mention his struggle and his family's plight over the years. It reported what it was told by the church.

Deacon Yoo's family didn't want the church funeral

service. Pastor Kim and most of the church members pleaded to have the farewell service in the church. They said he gave his life for the church, so he should be remembered by all the church people. Esther again conceded. The whole congregation and some neighbors came to the service. Lots of the mourners cried and hugged Esther and her daughters. They were filled with emotion. His family didn't go to the church after his death. They believed John Yoo was a real Christian.

When Ashley met Justin after her father's funeral, he was furious. He read about the tragic death of Ashley's father in the newspaper. Everything was beyond his comprehension. His family was Christian. Their church had a dwindling congregation. It didn't have an early morning Bible study. Why disrupt people's sleep? They can study the Bible on weekends. And most of his church members took their summer vacations. When they returned after summer people didn't ask, "Why didn't you come to church?" They asked, "How was your vacation?" Justin himself missed lots of church services. But he believed he was a Christian. The Christian spirit was in his soul.

His family didn't go to church every week, but they lived the Christian life. His family donated quite a lot of money to their church. They were not pushed. If the church had pressured them, they would not have given it. He thought that Koreans' faith was an aberration, almost crazy. He believed the church contributed to Ashley's father's death.

Ashley's family didn't want to accuse the church. It could cause severe damage to the church. And her father would never have wanted it. Her father was a true Christian, even though he was not a good father—ever since that fateful evening.

One night, Ashley sent a letter to Justin.

Dear Justin,

Thanks for everything. We visited my Dad's grave. It was a cloudless day. The sunshine radiated onto the memorial park and the gentle breeze soothed our pain. My Dad finally found peace and rest.

We placed a small white rose on his grave. My Dad was as pure as a white rose. He was a good Dad. There was another funeral procession in the park. Every day, people die. People should live a good life and end their lives in a meaningful way. My Dad couldn't. He thought he did, but I don't think so. The church thinks he died for God's work. We think we lost our beloved Dad. My Mom regained her composure and started to work again. Emily is doing well at school. Everything is settled now. Yesterday is history. We have tomorrow. It's another day. The forecast for the whole week is sunny. I will see you soon.

Love,
Ashley

Justin proposed to Ashley the next week and they got married. They married in an old and small church in Birmingham, Alabama, rather than in the big Korean church in Atlanta.

The Last Dinner

"Honey, read this letter. It's perplexing," said Young Kim to his wife.

"Who sent the letter? And what do you mean by perplexing?" Kate said.

"It's from Mr. Boklim Choi. He's inviting us to a dinner, but it's not a dinner like you would think. It sounds like 'The Last Supper,' a farewell dinner before his death."

"Really? That's unusual. Is he about to die? I didn't hear that he was sick. By the way, how old is he?"

"I guess he's in his mid-eighties."

"I also thought that. I haven't seen him in the last

few years. Nor have I ever heard he was seriously ill."

"You know, nobody can say anything about an old man's health. Circumstances can change at any time."

Young Kim handed the letter to his wife.

Dear friends,

I am inviting you to a dinner on Thursday, November 18, at Daedong Manor in Flushing, New York. It's intended to be for my family members and relatives, and also for my close friends. It is not my birthday or any other celebratory occasion. There's no denying that my final days are slowly approaching, but my days are not numbered. When I die, there will be no funeral service. I've already drawn up a will. My burial will be held in a quiet place on Long Island, attended only by my immediate family. I don't think I'll die soon, but my health has deteriorated this year. I just want to see you and say good-bye before it is too late.

Dinner and drinks will be served at 6 p.m. and the dress code is casual. Please do not bring gifts or flowers. Please accept my last invitation. See you then.

Yours sincerely,
Boklim Choi

Autumn in New York is too short. It arrives reluctantly, stays for a while, then runs away. The days preceding the dinner were bright, calm, and chilly. But on the morning of November 18, the weather forecast predicted a storm. The wind gusted at twenty mph and rain was on its way. The violent wind changed its direction and charged the innocent clouds like a galloping cavalry. Dark clouds gathered, and the rainstorm swept over the sky. The lonely trees looked desolate and trembled with fear under the threatening skies. The relentless storm made the trees miserable. Autumn bid its early adieu. People already felt frigid.

The days are especially brief in late November. As the year's end approached, it felt like the twilight of Boklim's life. The wind no longer whispered, but howled and chased the day with spears and arrows. The sky was a battlefield. As the hour approached six, people started to stream into the reception hall.

They complained it was so cold that it felt like winter. Some guests were bundled up in their winter coats, as if they not only wanted to shield themselves from the cold, but also from the bad news. The whole Choi family greeted guests. Boklim looked a bit tired, but not as though he was tired of living. He still had a good deal of energy. His complexion was good and he only had a modest amount of grey hair. He was standing firm and his shoulders didn't sag.

Erin, Boklim's first daughter, started to speak.

> Ladies and gentlemen, thank you for coming this evening. I hope the weather holds until we finish tonight's dinner. This is not a party, because we have nothing to celebrate. This occasion was made at my father's request. My Mom and us daughters all resisted, but he wanted to have this dinner, so we ultimately agreed. This is obviously an unusual dinner, but I believe it means a lot to my Dad and also for you.
>
> As some of you have probably noticed, he is not in good health. He spends most of his time by himself—reading, meditating, and writing. I have no idea what he is writing, but he sits for hours

in front of his computer. He loves to write. He is devoting his last days to creating poems, essays, and stories.

Dear friends, you are special. My Dad loves each of you. Please enjoy this dinner and have fun. Thank you. Dad, you are such a good father. I love you.

This outpouring of emotion drove some people to tears. Some wiped drifting tears with their handkerchiefs. A singer, soprano Yuri Park, ascended the stage and broke the silence. She delivered a song in a delicate, powerful voice. The lyrics came from one of Boklim's poems.

I wish my love to be a tree
Always standing there whenever I visit
When spring comes I wish she would rise from the frozen ground
In the stifling summer days I soothe my injured heart
With her broad and kind leaves
I wish she would be an ardent tree reddened with autumn leaves
Hanging on me in the fall
I wish she were a powerful tree enduring the punishing cold

With burning love for me during the long winter days
I hope she stays at the same place and cries for me looking over the sky
After I leave this beautiful world

Finishing her solo, Yuri hugged the songwriter. Her song was so touching and moving that for a moment people forgot to give her applause. Guests were in awe and were speechless. The lyrics were one of the most beloved poems that Boklim had ever created. Mr. Chirim Choi, Boklim's cousin, a drama professor at Joongang University in Korea, always read this poem whenever he officiated a wedding. He engraved this poem and gave it to the newlyweds, and they always cherished it.

Suddenly, thunder and lightening interrupted the proceedings. It was a perfect storm, written and performed by Mother Nature. Even though people couldn't see it, they felt its presence. It lasted for ten minutes.

Susan Choi, the second daughter, announced that dinner was ready.

Hello everybody. Some of you might be flustered tonight, but please don't worry. My Dad is a bit crazy, but I believe he is an honest man. Even though he has many faults in his personality, he always tries to address them. He is a very conscientious man. He knew he was selfish, but made amends with many acts of unselfishness.

My Dad gave me a job when I was in high school. It was my second job. My first job was delivering for Pennysavers. He owned a golf store at the time in K-town. He paid me in cash. I gave a good portion of my pay to the homeless near Penn Station. My Mom seemed surprised, but didn't say anything.

People who knew my Dad during this period might still harbor grudges against him. He had been unsmiling, impatient, rude, and not at all agreeable. I once heard somebody say he was an uncivilized man. I cannot dispute her opinion, but he became a different man. Now, he has a tender heart, cries often, and enjoys solitude.

If you've been offended by my Dad, please forgive him tonight. He has been bad on occasion, but he is mostly a good person.

Now the bar is open. Have as many drinks as you

want, but please be careful not to drink excessively. The police are very vigilant around here and they can sniff out alcohol.

Guests lined up for drinks. It was a cold night, but people were not in the mood to be drunk.

During dinner, three musicians, a pianist, and two cellists performed chamber music. Boklim and Jenny stopped by every table to thank them for their being there. People took pictures with their cameras and cell phones. They didn't say so, but they knew this would be the last image they would get. The atmosphere was generally somber. The Choi family tried to warm it. People smiled and cracked some jokes, but weren't in the mood to burst into laughter. It felt like a funeral, not for a dead person, but for someone still alive.

After dinner, Jay Lee, a former president of the Korean American Scholarship Foundation, mounted the podium.

Ladies and gentlemen, I am exceedingly happy tonight to talk about Mr. Choi. He served two years as president of KASF, and another two years as vice president under me. I can say without hesitation that he truly was one of the best presidents we've ever had. If he were a selfish man, he would not have accepted his vice-presidency. He worked really hard, was very responsible, constantly thought about our foundation, and suggested novel ideas for the organization. He had a mission, and took on a daunting task.

I clearly remember what he said when he first joined as a new member. He said he couldn't have graduated college without a scholarship. He wanted to give back for what he had received, paying it forward to the next generation. Actually, he contributed a lot more money and effort than he had ever received himself.

Dear friends of Mr. Choi, I would like to present a video he personally wrote and oversaw.

(A video is played of an old couple walking together in a beach park at dusk.)

Narrator: You've walked a long way. Now is the time to sit on a bench and take a rest. You deserve it, for you've worked so hard in your life. When you left Korea, your motherland was very poor and had high unemployment. At that time, leaving Korea itself was "patriotic." You have been a successful immigrant. You've achieved a great deal and, most importantly, you've raised your children to be great successes. Now we have to think about the future generations. What will you leave for them?

KASF is launching a ten million dollar fundraising campaign. We have an endowment of five million dollars now. We need that much more. Many of the first generation immigrants are at the twilight of their lives. The sun will rise again tomorrow morning, but "we won't." What will you leave for the next generation? Please talk to your family members and leave a small portion of your legacy for KASF. Thank you.

Jay Lee took a microphone and said in a compelling voice:

Dear friends, I have two important announcements this evening. Mr. Choi is not a rich man, but his family decided to donate fifty thousand dollars to KASF. Fortunately, my apparel business has been doing well, so I'll donate 300,000 dollars to KASF. I've already talked to my daughters and they wholeheartedly agreed.

Mr. Choi and I believe that helping the future generation is the best legacy we can pass on. I know him. He may not be a great man, but he is a man of compassion. I wish for him to live many more years to impact more people. Thank you.

The next speaker was poet Jeongki Kim, who had been his poetry teacher for the last twenty years. She could barely walk and ascended the podium with the assistance of a student. She was noticeably weak and spoke in a feeble voice.

I somehow lived long enough to have this moment. When Boklim suggested this strange night, I didn't believe it. He is a courageous man in a sense. My husband passed away about twenty years ago. Boklim and his wife were two of the last people who had seen him. My husband's passing was a huge loss for me. The world will miss his extraordinary knowledge on Korean history. My mobility stopped with his death. I can't drive. He always brought me wherever I had to go.

Mr. Choi has been a journalist-writer. He has a keen sense of observation, and he knows how to find the right word. He's been brutally honest about himself, especially in his writing. He knew he was not a poet at the level he wanted to be. He was talented, but a humble prose and verse creator. His poems were pure and musical. He wrote poems and essays both in Korean and English. It's never easy. He spent hours and hours studying English and ultimately reached a point where he was able to publish a collection of his short stories in English. I believe he is a good communicator. He had been a good broadcaster and writer.

As a poetry teacher I used to speak highly of my students, even when I found faults. I didn't have to say anything to him. He knew his problems, and fixed them quickly. He and I believe the best legacy we can leave is our literary work. We will be gone soon or not too soon. Please find one poem or essay you like and read it again.

I don't know who will die first. The order may not

be that significant. We will leave this world, but our literary works remain. I hope he outlives me. If you had any misgiving about us, please forgive us. You can hate him, but you cannot hate his writing.

Good night, everybody. Boklim gave me an opportunity to talk about myself as well. Thank you.

More students helped her sit down. She seemed tired but content. She was the mother of all her students and always took good care of them. Nobody else could do a better job.

Stacey, Boklim's third daughter, spoke next.

My Dad is a unique person. Honestly, I couldn't believe he could write. As an English major at Dartmouth I knew how hard writing was. When he mentioned writing in English, I thought he was joking. He wasn't born here, his pronunciation was not accurate, and sometimes he made simple mistakes. I'm sorry, Dad, I really thought so. I underestimated his talent.

I saw he was buying books from Barnes and Noble. Whenever I went home I saw new books. He

> was serious. Many years ago, he showed me a short story. I thought it was a joke. It wasn't. It was better than I expected. It was good. He had hesitated to ask me to read his work. I realized getting help from his daughter was very difficult. I'm sorry, Dad. I was willing to help you.
>
> Lots of people say I'm like my Dad. I resemble him most, and my Mom said that our personalities are similar.
>
> Ladies and gentlemen, look at us closely and compare us. I have no idea how he conceived this crazy thought about having this dinner. It's a farewell party prior to his departure from this world. But I came to realize that this might be a great idea. It is the epitome of who he is because he always thinks differently. I think he has a lot to tell you. I hope he doesn't go too far. Dad, can you promise me not to go too crazy?

People laughed. They took a picture of them. Stacey introduced him to the crowd: "Ladies and gentlemen, here's my Dad."

Guests stood up and greeted him as he made his way back to the podium.

Dear friends, both of my parents passed away at eighty-five. People live longer now, but in my parents' time, it was a long life. Unfortunately, my eldest brother died at fifty-five, my third brother at sixty-five, and second brother died at eighty-two. I happen to be the only one still living among my four brothers. There's no question I'll be next. During my life, I have gone to many funerals. It's part of life. People always die. I have even witnessed people dying. They looked awful. The dead person didn't know I was there. They couldn't see people coming to express sympathy. There's no way they could hear people crying. I realized it was meaningless. My mother-in-law is resting in peace at Pine Lawn Memorial Park. My wife often visits her. Sometimes I go with her. One day I came across a familiar name there. He was an accountant and music critic. I hadn't heard he was dead.

Dear friends, I really don't want you to see my dead body. I am a selfish man. It's too much for me. You can accuse me or even slap my face now if you have any grievance against me. You can claim any money, if I owe you. You can say good words to me while I breathe. Everything has to be addressed while I live. When I pass away, there'll be no funeral. Not to save money, but to save face. I will be buried in a quiet place in Pine Lawn. I asked my family not to burn me.

My condition is not terribly bad now. I can still breathe and, most importantly, I can think. My imagination is very much alive, although my heart says my final days are nearing. I think parting with this world is a kind of concession. I am an old passenger in a packed bus. If I depart and vacate a seat, the bus can take another passenger. I am ready to give my seat to a new passenger.

My life has been a failure. There have been few successes and numerous mistakes. I've never been a good husband. I am deeply apologetic to my wife. Fortunately, she will live longer than me. By dying, I can give her freedom. I have been selfish. She was the greatest victim of my super ego.

I was born poor. My father stammered in his speech. He could not survive hard times and made my family poor. My mother was a good-natured woman but uneducated. She couldn't read. I was the only one who finished college.

My childhood days and college years were

miserable. I would not have graduated from college without a Korean government loan. I came to this country before I paid off my loan. This made me join KASF. I worked hard to pay back what I received for the next generation. My poverty in youth made me a pessimistic person. I have a tendency to prepare for the worst. I was nervous, impatient, very selfish, and unfriendly to others. I was a loner. I have been kind of disagreeable.

As my economic condition improved, I began to realize that I had to be a better man. I am a pensive, almost brooding type of man. I knew what my faults were and began to address them. Those of you who met me in the past two decades found me to be a decent guy. I have improved much and I am almost a different man. I know one lady here who used to say I was not a civilized man, back when I was middle-aged. I was initially mad, but I've accepted it. She is here. Please forgive me now. My wish is that tonight becomes a day of reconciliation and forgiveness. I sincerely apologize for my past misbehavior.

I once made a poem describing my life as a balance sheet. I used a metaphor. I didn't know much about accounting, but I figured my good deeds are in the plus column and something bad goes to the minus column. I tried hard to make my balance sheet end in a surplus. I am hoping tonight's event makes up for past mistakes and puts my life in the plus column.

I don't believe I have been a good writer. At the end of every year, I reflect upon the poems, essays, and short stories that I produced during the year. I was seldom satisfied. I felt sorry for them. Sometimes I felt like I showed contempt for literature. If any of you liked my work, I would be very happy. Whether good or bad, my literary works are the legacy I leave in this world. Looking back at my life, I was the worst husband, a not-so-good father, and not a good friend. Please forgive me. I tried to transform myself from being perfectly selfish to less selfish, and to ultimately become a selfless man, but I've fallen short. Now, if you have any questions about my life, please ask me now, before it's too late. Thank you.

An almost-seventy-year-old woman approached Boklim and handed him an envelope. "Mr. Choi, I borrowed thirty dollars from you seventeen years ago. Here is the money."

"Thirty dollars? I lent you money seventeen years ago? I have no recollection."

"I don't blame you. We, the New York–New Jersey literature class, went to visit Edgar Allen Poe's cottage in July and we had a barbecue afterward. I borrowed thirty dollars from you. I forgot about it for a while. Suddenly, I remembered and I wondered if you had also forgotten. I waited for you to mention it, but you never did. Eventually, I realized that my thoughts kept coming back to you, because I owed you money. That's why it's taken me so long to pay you."

"Actually, I didn't forget. But it was such a small amount of money that I didn't bother you. I'll give you back this money. Hopefully you will keep thinking of me until my final day."

Boklim didn't take the money.

"No, Mr. Choi, you should take it." People laughed. Boklim took the money reluctantly.

"You will remain in our hearts. We, the literature classmates, love you. You have been a great help," she said.

Mr. Sung Kim stood up and asked him a question. "Mr. Choi, you came to church for a long time and suddenly stopped coming. What made you do that?"

"That is an awkward question, but I'll answer. I have no fear in keeping the truth from you at this stage of my life. I don't believe in God. Not only Jesus—any God. I know many of you won't agree with me, and some of you may even hate me for saying this. I didn't want to be a hypocrite. I don't believe in Jesus's resurrection and his second coming. However, I have full respect for others' faith. I think science and our modern lifestyles have changed people's faith. I see fewer and fewer people going to church these days. I don't consider myself a good writer, but I believe writers have more doubts about the existence of God. I once believed each individual was the center of world. When people die, that's the end of their world."

Another man asked him a question. "Mr. Choi, there are a good number of people here tonight. Did you invite only your very closest friends?"

"I consider everyone friends, but some are not my real friends. There's one gentleman here that I didn't like at all at one point. An incident occurred about twenty-five years ago that made me really angry. I apologize for my narrow-mindedness. I have been a stubborn man, but as I said earlier, I became more open and generous in my later years. I know some of you don't like me for various reasons. That's okay. We can reconcile tonight. I really don't want to die with hatred or being hated by anyone."

A person from New Jersey added, "I am a big fan of your essays. You seemed to seek a pure love through your writing. Have you found one or do you think you can get one in the after-world?"

"I don't believe in eternal life. As soon as I die, I am just a dead body. It's like a dead rabbit or a dead tree.

"Yes, I was looking for a pure love. When I was very young, I was close to finding one. As I got older it became almost impossible. Love is beautiful, but pure love is hard to acquire."

The last comment came from an old friend of his. "Mr. Choi, I am very concerned about you after tonight. Will you go into hiding? When can I see you again?"

"You won't see me again. I won't be home. I'll be

traveling around Korea and throughout the United States. I want to meet as many people as possible. I will trace my footprints until my last moment. I will be a forgotten man. You will not hear of my death either."

Dinner was over. Guests lingered for a while. People tried to talk with him, one last time. Some cried, as if it were a funeral. The storm was over. The sky cleared to reveal a half moon. The gentle breeze washed away people's anxiety. Everybody headed home. Only he stayed. It was his last dinner with friends he would never see again. He would disappear and become an invisible man.

Eight months passed after the dinner. A small local newspaper in Albany, New York, reported a car accident. An old man's body was discovered in the Catskill Valley. The gas tank was empty. The driver committed suicide with his 250,000-mile Toyota Avalon. It was Boklim's beloved car. The car died with him. There was a white blanket in the back seat. There was his address and home phone number. Police had no doubt that it was a suicide.

His body was handed over to his family and buried in Pine Lawn. The local Korean newspaper reported his death. Some of his friends visited the cemetery. They found his grave. His poem from the party was inscribed in his headstone. He was resting in peace.

His poem said that a tree stood there crying, waiting for him to look up the sky. No tree was there. He always wanted to die the way he wanted. He didn't want to be forced to die. But he couldn't control what happened after he died. The memorial park wouldn't allow a tree to be planted by his gravesite.

Author's Note

It wasn't easy. It was a daunting task for me. Lots of my friends might wonder about the making of this book.

Can he do it? Is his English good enough? These are all legitimate questions. I doubted myself too. But I ultimately did it. It may not be as good as I wanted, but I made it.

I basically believe someone who writes poems, essays, and novels in his/her own language can write them in another language. A language is a tool. People can have tools and get used to them. It depends how hard he/she tries. I came to the United States in my late 20s. I have been reading *The New York Times* for the last thirty-five years, and I am a member of three English book clubs. I read about one thousand pages a month. I don't just read the books; I read them very carefully. I analyze the sentences and always make notes. I also went to night school to learn how to write fiction. Is that enough? Probably not. My family was the first to express their doubts. They thought I was either stupid or crazy. As time passed, they found I was very serious and determined. Then they started to help me. My daughters read the first drafts and edited them. They complained, but they did it. I also thank my wife. She questioned why I wrote in English and bothered the girls at first, but she soon realized she couldn't stop me.

I owe a lot to my literary friends: Adrienne Leslie, Sandra Foley, Cristal Kim, Yong Shin, and Bokyon Kim. They kindly read my drafts and encouraged me, especially Adrienne, who spent hours with me. She not only edited my stories but gave me invaluable advice. My Korean friends and teachers, Dr. Chonggi Mah and poet Jeongki Kim, gave me good feedback and told me to "keep going." I am deeply appreciative of you all. I cannot express enough gratitude to Donna Deedy. Her husband, Paul Deedy, is a Titleist salesman. He told me his father was a writer and a good friend of John Updike. He also told me his wife was a freelance writer who contributed to *The New*

York Times. She kindly read my stories and edited them. I also thank my literature classmates and book club members. They are all book lovers.

Meeting Hank Kim, the CEO of Seoul Selection, resulted in a dramatic turn of events. Seoul Selection was the publishing company in my mind from the beginning, but they were hard to reach. I tried to make contact through email, phone calls, and other means. Nobody helped me. Then, one day it suddenly clicked. Hank responded to me from California. I was going to travel to Los Angeles on that day to attend the annual directors' meeting of Korean American Scholarship Foundation as a delegate of the NY Chapter. We sat together and talked not only about my book, but literature in general. It was like meeting an old friend unexpectedly. I was very fortunate to meet him. Hank and his editorial staff reviewed the manuscript and offered many fine suggestions and essential corrections.

Boklim Choi

Boklim Choi is a journalist-writer. He worked for over twenty years in print media and broadcasting in the United States and Korea. He has published two poetry collections and two novels in Korean. He has also published a golf essay collection and still contributes essays to a Korean paper. This is his first collection of short stories in English. He was born and raised in Korea. He graduated from Yonsei University in Seoul and received his Master's degree in communications from City University of New York. He lives in Port Washington, New York, with his wife. He has three grown daughters.

Credits

Publisher	Kim Hyunggeun
Editor	Kim Hansol
Copy editors	Felix Im, Jaime Stief
Designer	Jung Hyun-young
Cover illustrator	Miwoo